Taming Evil

John Sturgeon

Black Rose Writing | Texas

ISBN: 978-1-68433-693-7
PUBLISHED BY BLACK ROSE WRITING
www.blackrosewriting.com

Printed in the United States of America
Suggested Retail Price (SRP) $18.95

Taming Evil is printed in Palatino Linotype

*As a planet-friendly publisher, Black Rose Writing does its best to eliminate
unnecessary waste to reduce paper usage and energy costs, while never
compromising the reading experience. As a result, the final word count vs. page count
may not meet common expectations.

"If an injury has to be done to a man it should be so severe his
vengeance need not be feared."

MACHIAVELLI

Taming Evil

Day One

They found me at The Bitter End, a rundown dump over in the Bed Bug Row area. When I awoke from my sleep I wasn't as close to the end as I felt. There was a nasty stabbing pain at both temples and the light from the new day made everything more sensitive. My body felt like it did after one of those long boxing workouts at Holy Trinity with Father Luigi; everything ached. My tongue and mouth tasted like I had been fed dirt. There was no moisture in it. My nose appeared to be fine; I could smell everything in the Godforsaken room from perspiration to piss to vomit. My ears were working, too. I heard the voices mentioning my name, telling me to wake up, trying to tell me that there was something important that needed to be done. I wanted everything and everyone to be gone. That must have been why I closed my eyes. This response was not wise. The owners of the voices I'd heard hit me with a bucket of icy, cold water. I would have rather been electrocuted. Then I would have been dead. As it was, I came off the bed a bit like I'd been shot out of a cannon.

"Son of a bitch, "I yelled. Now my head, aided by the jerking motion, really hurt. My eyes, not entirely focused, settled on two shadows in the room.

"Fits no one in this room, except maybe you," said one of the voices.

I tried to gain my balance and sit up in the bed, but this was truly a Herculean effort. Again I flirted with the idea of being dead.

"Patrick," said a soothing voice, "we need you to get up and out of that bed and out of this room. We need your help."

I did manage to sit up and immediately rubbed at the nagging temples. I asked for water and someone gave me a glass. I drank it down, erasing some of the grit in my mouth. I tried to focus again on the shadows, but that blur was still there.

"Worse than what you saw in New York?" the first voice said.

"Much, much," said the second. "He was able to stand very soon after I saw him."

"Not likely here."

I rubbed at my temples and eyes and finally was able to get them open. The room wasn't that light, indicating maybe it was early morning. Vision returned slowly and painfully.

"Moses, there are enough people in this city who would probably love to see you dead. Why must you take it upon yourself to try and do their work for them?"

Eyesight restored, I turned towards this voice. George Loftus was standing to my right, holding, I hoped, an empty bucket. To his right, a little behind Loftus, was the short figure of Harold Pinter, the criminologist who I thought was my friend.

"Patrick, I am sorry that we had to track you down and to douse you with water," Harold said, "but word had come that it seemed that your goal was oblivion. We just couldn't have that and then a pressing matter came along, one that requires your assistance."

I put up one finger to silence Harold. I took a deep breath and instantly wished I hadn't. Fresh air was not present in this room. "Where am I?"

"The fucking Bitter End of all places," Loftus said.

"Bed Bug Row," I mumbled. "How long?"

"Three days," Harold said. "We heard some lawyer representing the Farmer girl came into the precinct to meet with you. After the meeting, you walked out of the front door and this is where we found you."

"How?"

"The madam, Mrs. Flint, got tired of bringing whiskey bottles to you. It was more that she got tired of you throwing the empty bottles against walls and mirrors in her fine establishment." Loftus jerked a thumb over his shoulder at a broken mirror above a cheap dresser.

"The girls were also becoming a bit frightened," Harold said. "They wouldn't come into the room any longer."

"I didn't hurt anyone, did I?"

"Not physically, but apparently you have taught the young ladies some new descriptions for their profession; most they will not repeat," Loftus said.

I winced. "So what happened?"

"In one of your more sane moments you told one of the girls that you would shoot her in the head if she, or any of her cohorts, stole any of your belongings. When you were passed out they checked and found your identification and your revolver, which they did confiscate for their and your own good. Mrs. Flint called us when she reached her limit."

"Jesus," I muttered.

"He's not going to help you out here, Moses," Loftus said.

Seeing Loftus triggered something in my feeble brain. "Those two girls, Patricia Farmer and Madeline Marsden, are guilty aren't they, George?"

Loftus shrugged. "We all heard what you heard. They killed those three old women. That makes them guilty, but now they both have lawyers."

The pasty face of Bradley Luke popped into my head. His face and a remembrance of what he had told me about Patricia Farmer not being guilty. "Both girls behind bars?"

"Both girls are being held in the Cook County Home for Wayward Children."

I shook my head at this. These girls were both wayward, but it was the attorney Luke's words that sent me on my little bender.

"We need you to come with us," Harold said. "Of course, you'll have to clean up a bit."

All of the smells I described earlier were coming from me or from nearby me. "I need some time to get my head straight, to clean up and get some decent clothes."

"Shipley thinks the three days that you went missing is enough of a vacation so time is not a commodity that you have a lot of," Loftus said.

I rubbed my head again. "What is the rush this time?"

Harold stepped closer to the bed. In the dim light of the room he looked particularly pale and tired. "There has been a murder," he said quietly.

"A murder?" I asked. There were always murders in the Levee.

"Not singular, Moses," Loftus said. "Four murders. Ever hear the name Allen Price, a big shot at the commodities exchange."

"Can't say that I have."

"Me neither, until about two hours ago. Somebody entered Mr. Price's house sometime in the past two days and shot most of his head off with a shotgun."

I swallowed hard. "You said four murders."

Loftus nodded as Harold hung his head. "Whoever it was killed Mrs. Price, their fourteen year old son Daniel and their sixteen year old daughter Rachel. All killed with a shotgun, close range, very thorough and violent."

I felt nauseous for moment and fought back the urge to vomit. "Clues?" I managed to ask.

Loftus smiled weakly. "Not a one."

•   •   •

Before leaving The Bitter End I apologized to Mrs. Flint and any of the girls who were around. None of them smiled, but I did get a smirk from the madam when I gave her a twenty dollar bill. I won't say I felt better, but it helped to go to my apartment first, clean up and get some fresh clothes. On the way out I thought about Lois Winston and little Freddie, long gone from Chicago. I hoped they were far enough away. As we passed the first floor apartment, Loftus pointed at the unit.

"Somebody shot the superintendent dead in his apartment," he said. "Happened the day before you left. Any ideas?"

I looked at the closed door. "None," I said.

"Like most things in this fucking city," he said.

The building they drove me to on 39th Street was a three story brownstone. The front area was neat, all the plants and lawn trimmed nicely. There were about ten steps that led up to a porch fronting the building. At the top of the steps stood a tall, overweight cop. He looked like he was close to passing out. As the day neared noon, the temperature was close to ninety and the humidity was stifling. Even though I'd cleaned up, my shirt was sticking to me under my suit coat.

Loftus led the way up the stairs and pushed open the door of the apartment. The heat in the house was hotter and there was no air circulation. As Harold and I followed George into the unit the first thing I noticed was that everything had been turned over, pulled out and torn apart. The living room that I first saw had every cushion from every chair or couch slashed open; stuffing was everywhere. Anything that had drawers, had them pulled out and emptied on the floor. Books were lying everywhere, the shelves that they belonged to were empty. Pictures that had been hanging on the walls were now lying on the floor, some smashed.

"A robbery," I said.

"Gone bad," Harold noted.

"Brilliant deduction, Mr. Holmes," Loftus chided. "Follow me."

We followed George into a large office just past the living room. This room was mostly a large, ornate desk, expensive chair and wall to wall bookshelves. The desk drawers had all been emptied out and every book was on the floor, exposing bear walls where they had been. On the floor, behind the desk, lay the body of Allen Price. He still wore his suit pants, white shirt and vest; I didn't see his jacket anywhere. I also didn't see much of Mr. Price's head. Whoever killed him blew most of it off. This was mostly on the carpet and shelves about fifteen feet from the victim.

"What the hell were they after?" I asked. "What made them so mad to tear this place apart and then kill Price in this fashion?"

"Something pretty big," Loftus said. "Something I don't think they ever found."

We walked out of the office towards the kitchen. Only a few feet into the kitchen lay the body of a woman. This would be Mrs. Price. She was lying on her stomach. I could see on the floor leading into the kitchen and in the entry way a trail of blood. Closer examination showed that she had been hit with a shotgun blast in the center of her back. This hadn't killed her. The holes in the back of her head indicated that a small caliber revolver had finished the deed.

"I think she saw the gunmen shoot her husband in the office and she tried to run this way, down the hallway," Loftus said. "She was shot in the back and then crawled a few feet before they caught up with her. You can see from the head wounds what followed."

I nodded and looked around the kitchen. Every bowl, plate, pan, saucer, cup and piece of silver were strewn about the floor. Every cabinet in the big kitchen had been torn open and emptied. "So Price wouldn't tell them where what they were looking for was located so they shot him. Mrs. Price runs down the hall, they shoot her and then tear the kitchen apart."

"They didn't find it here either," Harold says.

"You need to see upstairs," Loftus said.

There was a winding staircase before you got to the kitchen that led to the second floor. On the way up I could see where two pictures had last resided. Their hooks and nails were still in place, but the pictures had been torn down and now lay on the stairs. The first room I was shown was the master where the parents slept. Staying with the pattern, the intruders had torn the room apart. There wasn't an inch of the floor that wasn't covered with the past contents of drawers, closet or bureau. The sheets and blankets had been torn from the bed, the mattress was askew.

The second bedroom was that of the daughter. It too was torn apart and the bed had been stripped and checked. The difference here was that the girl, aged 17, was lying on top of the bed, hands, mouth and feet tied. Her head was splattered all over the bed and pillow. That was it for me. The nausea hit me and I turned to puke, but nothing came up. My ribs might as well have been hit by a heavyweight. The gagging almost dizzied me; I broke a sweat.

"You going to be okay, Patrick," Harold said. His hand was resting on my shoulder.

"No," I said honestly. I stood and looked at Loftus. He had lit a cigarette and suddenly I wanted one. "I assume the boy is in the same shape?"

"Just like the girl," George said. "Tied and blown apart."

"What's on the upper level?"

"A sizeable space, unfinished, used for storage. Everything up there was torn apart. The whole house, every damn inch, torn apart."

"With the pictures torn down, I get the idea that maybe they were looking for a wall safe. When they found none they just tore everything apart."

"That's kind of what I thought, but who knows."

"Anything missing?"

Loftus shrugged. "Can't say. The killers may have eventually got what they were looking for."

"Who called this in?"

"Dairy delivery man. Got here about four-thirty. Front door was wide open and the office light was on. He took one step inside and called us from the call box on the corner."

"So nothing?"

"I wouldn't say nothing. We have a fairly prominent Chicago businessman, his wife and two kids shot gunned to death and their house torn apart. We just don't have a motive or any idea why or who."

"Harold?"

"We need the coroner to claim the bodies and maybe remove any remnants of shells and certainly the bullets in Mrs. Price's head. Some examination of the bullet fragments may help later. Once the bodies are gone I can begin to go through the house and everything that's been tossed around. It shouldn't be that hard to find finger prints. The killer or killers seemed to have touched everything."

I nodded. "Where do we start, George?"

"You know the drill, Moses. Talk to everyone who knew the victims. Talk to all the neighbors. Somebody heard or saw something. For some reason the killers had an idea there was something of great value in this house."

"Then that's where we start," I said.

"Not quite, Moses," George said. "Lieutenant Shipley would like a word with you. He has some questions about your recent disappearance, the Farmer/Marsden case and why Jack Garfield wants you suspended. We have to see him as soon as you feel up to it. Would that be now?"

I never felt that there was a good time to face Shipley. "Now is as good a time as any."

•   •   •

"You picked an odd time to go on a sabbatical, Detective Moses," Lieutenant Shipley said from behind his desk on the second floor of the 22nd Precinct building.

"I don't know if I'd call it a sabbatical, sir. I needed a few days away. That's all.

Shipley stretched his neck under the shirt collar that was always too tight. "You were gone three days," his high pitched voice shrieked. "From what I understand you were holed up in some Bed Bug Row brothel."

"I wasn't having such a good time, sir."

"And I suppose everyone else that works out of this precinct and in this ward is just having a grand old time?"

I realized for the first time since Loftus and Harold located me that I was very hungry. "I would imagine that everyone else is having about as much fun as I was."

"We have these two girls who have murdered three old women and now we have a family of four shot to death in their own home. Your timing wasn't very good."

"I am sorry, sir. I meant no disrespect to you or the department."

His look told me how surprised he was by my comment. I wasn't sure he believed me. "You are also aware that someone put a bullet into the forehead of the landlord of your building? This seems to have happened the day that you went missing."

"Detective Loftus made me aware of that crime this morning."

"And a man by the name of William Winston, missing since March, was dug up in the backyard of the home he once occupied with his wife and young son. The coroner says he was bludgeoned to death and then buried."

"I don't know anything about the case."

"But what about his poor widow and the young boy? Records indicate that Lois Winston and her son, Freddie, last occupied the apartment across from yours."

"I know Lois and Freddie."

"Any idea where they are?"

"I didn't even know they were gone."

"It appears they left town the same day you went away, which as we discussed, was the same day that the poor landlord met his demise."

I tried to look aghast. "You don't think Lois Winston killed the landlord?"

Shipley rolled his eyes and then loosened his shoulders. "The landlord murder is a mystery. What I don't think is a mystery is that William Winston's body was discovered after a detective fitting your description was asking questions about him days before his body was found."

"So you do think Lois killed her husband?"

"Please don't play coy with me, Moses. You know I am a man of little humor."

I took a deep breath. "William Winston was beating his wife. Lois, in total defense of herself, killed him. With the help of Freddie, she dragged the body to the berm in her backyard and buried it. I discovered this after a little snooping around. I confronted her with my little tale and apparently, after admitting the crime, she left town. This all happened the day after we caught Madeline Marsden and Patricia Farmer. We were a little busy with that case and I guess I waited too long to turn Lois in."

"And no idea where she went?"

"None."

Shipley managed a small smile. "The next time you discover a murderess in our midst would you put your vacation plans on hold for a moment and either turn her in or arrest her?"

"I understand, sir."

"The Price murders will now take up most of your time. I don't think Chief Collins or the mayor will be too excited when the details of that crime hit the papers today. I would imagine I will hear from someone at headquarters later on."

"And Marsden and Farmer?"

"Both girl's families have hired lawyers. From what I hear, the Farmer girl says she was just there, somewhat ignorantly, and was a spectator. Her lawyer is claiming she did nothing physical to the women. That seems to be their defense."

"That story seems like horseshit. What are we to do?"

"Let's see how this plays out. I don't like it when lawyers get involved, but remember if we get a conviction of any kind that may be the best we can do."

I didn't agree with Shipley entirely, thinking of the comments the lawyer Bradley Luke had made.

"And Moses, can we try and keep on the right track for just a bit while these investigations continue? There are still some in headquarters who do not believe you should be working for the department. I don't agree with that assessment, but I am a small fish in a big pond."

I didn't need Shipley to tell me who. "I will do my best, sir."

He shook his head slowly. "You are excused, Moses."

• • •

I couldn't find Loftus or Riley O'Donnell when I left Shipley's office. I checked downstairs, but Harold Pinter wasn't around either. It was close to noon and it was obvious that vicious crimes didn't get in the way of lunchtime. It seemed everyone that I needed to talk with had vanished from the precinct building.

It didn't matter if it was lunch or dinner, the beer was always a little warm and the food was still marginal at Cooper's. I needed a beer or two to right the ship a bit and I had some dried beef with potatoes. In the middle of the second beer the pain that had been dwelling in my temples abated a bit. The food, as bad as it was, took care of the hunger. What neither did was answer any of my questions and there were plenty of those.

We had all heard Madeline Marsden and Patricia Farmer tell us how they had killed the three older women. We had heard the motive, defeating boredom and committing a crime the cops couldn't solve, and the detailed way they killed the women. Madeline, when arrested, took the blame for the entire caper. She said that Patricia wasn't responsible for anything. This baffled me. It was clear that both girls had thought up the crime and were accomplices. Why Madeline would say that she was solely responsible for the murders was crazy. There was something going on there and I intended to find out what it was. I also intended to prove that Bradley Luke's comments were not accurate. If Patricia Farmer was guilty at all she was going to pay for it.

It seemed to me that Shipley wasn't going to press me much on Lois Winston. I had told him what I knew, but wasn't quite honest about the timing of my discovery of the murderer and when I could have turned her in. Maybe Shipley agreed with my assessment that William deserved what he got and that Lois had gone through hell at some time and was now gone. I was good with that and hoped he didn't bring it up again.

My two enemies Captain Garfield and Christian Hanson were still out there. Both still seemed to be looking for me. One was responsible for Mr. Burkhart's, the landlord's murder, during the abduction of Freddie Winston. Danger was definitely still afoot and I would have to be aware of what was going on. It would help if I could stay sober and alert.

My newest assignment, the robbery and murder of a family of four was too new to even begin to reason about. Somebody was looking for something in the Price residence. Everything indicated they didn't find it and the killers decided to kill everyone on site. What the killers were after would lead us to why the family was killed. Until we discovered that we had nothing. The only clue seemed to be that Allen Price was successful in the commodities markets. This, I thought rather glumly, led me to very little.

•   •   •

Loftus and I thought the best place to start was with the Price's neighbors. The next door neighbor to the west lived in a nice brownstone like the Prices. The two buildings could have been twins. There was no shortage of wealth on this block; that was clear. We didn't have any idea who resided in the adjoining properties. That didn't matter. We only hoped they could tell us something about the Prices and who may have murdered them.

We pounded on the door of the first neighbor. We waited a bit and pounded again. There was a slight movement of a curtain in the window. Someone briefly glanced at who was banging on their door.

"Probably thinks we're the murderers," Loftus said.

"Can't blame them."

Loftus took out his badge and faced it towards the window. He banged on the door again with his free hand. The curtain nudged again. In a moment the door was opened by a small woman, gray haired with circular glasses. She looked like America's grandmother.

"Can I help you?" she said.

"We are with the police," Loftus said. "I'm Detective Loftus. This is Detective Moses. We'd like to ask you a couple of questions about your neighbors, the Prices."

Her eyes shifted to the right towards the Price's residence. "That's a terrible thing, especially in this neighborhood."

"Yes it is," George said. "May we come in for a moment?"

She let us enter her house and it was clear that nothing in the place had changed in twenty years. Everything was old and there was a lot of dust. It appeared to me that our host was wearing an old dress. There was some spots of repair stitching and a few from wear and tear. The chairs we sat in were ancient. Dust rose from them as we sat. There might be wealth in the neighborhood, but it might have run dry in this house.

"What is your name?" I asked.

"You don't look well," she said.

"Summer influenza. Nasty stuff," I said.

"My name is Samantha Browning."

"Is there a Mr. Browning?"

"There was, but he has been dead for over ten years. I live here alone."

I nodded. "Did you know the Prices very well?"

"I am not surprised that somebody murdered him," she said bluntly.

I looked at George; he shrugged. "Mrs. Browning, are you aware that the whole family has been murdered, not just Mr. Price?"

She waved a hand at me. "I would speak a lot with Louise when I saw her. She was a very nice woman; her children were very nice and pleasant." She stopped and looked towards the back of the house. "I could brew some tea if you would like."

"That's nice, but we're fine. You were talking about the Prices."

"Yes," she said. "I would talk to Louise and she would tell me things. They weren't nice things. I'm not sure I should tell you."

"Mrs. Browning," George said, "we are investigating a multiple murder. Right now, we have little to go on. We need to hear whatever it is that you can tell us."

Her eyes went from George to me and back and forth a few times. She looked nervous, scared.

"You said you weren't surprised that somebody murdered him," I said. "I assume you meant Allen Price. Why would you say that?"

"Excuse my French, but Allen Price was a bastard. Louise would tell me of his demanding, controlling ways with her and the children. She told me he was a tyrant with a terrible temper. She was afraid of him."

"That's good to know, but Mrs. Price was murdered as well, the children, too," George said.

She returned her gaze to me. "If you'll ask a few questions, you'll find that Allen Price practiced the same tyrannical behavior in the business world. He was mean to employees and clients alike. He was apparently not nice to anyone. It wouldn't surprise me that there is a long list of people who wouldn't mind if he was murdered and another list of those who would probably do it.

"I heard their house was torn apart. This was done to make it look like a robbery. There is no doubt that this was just a prop to cover the murder. The goal of this crime was to kill Allen Price. If you follow the robbery angle you'll be going in the wrong direction. Look at Allen Price. That will give you the clues you need to find the killers.

As we left Mrs. Browning and her dusty home I knew that Loftus and I had a different feeling about the Price murders. Was the family murdered during a robbery or was that just a ruse?

"A bit of a daffy woman," George said, "but she seems pretty clear on Price.

"I don't think we can sway her in any other direction."

"We'd better talk to the neighbor on the other side."

"Confirming what Mrs. Browning said will help give us a few leads."

"According to her, they'll be many."

From our little talk, if it was true, that was an understatement. I saw little reason to respond.

The door to the house on the east was opened by a black woman adorned in a maid's uniform. She was a middle aged woman, slender with her black hair hidden under a blue hat. He stern look told us she wasn't happy to see us. "Mr. Rudd is in the loop on business and Mrs. Rudd has taken the children out for the afternoon," she said.

"Who might you be?" I asked.

"I might be Ms. Wilma Carruthers," she said and then she smiled. "How can I help you?"

"We were looking to talk with the owners of this house, but maybe you can help us," I said. "Can you tell us anything about the Prices, the people next door?"

For a moment she seemed a little nervous. I thought she might get wet feet about saying anything to us. Her eyes looked up and down the street. "I really enjoy my job here working for the Rudds," she said.

"I wouldn't want to do anything that would get me in any trouble with them."

"Whatever you tell us will be held in confidence," I countered.

"Mrs. Rudd would talk with Mrs. Price on a regular basis. I wouldn't call them friends, but they were very neighborly. Mrs. Rudd would tell me things because she was worried."

"Worried about what?" George said, prodding.

She gave him a hard look. "I'm trying to get there. She was very worried that something was actually going to happen to Mrs. Price. She thought Mr. Price was a terrible man; he was very mean to his wife. He wasn't very nice to his children. He was also a meaner person when he drank which I understand was on a very regular basis."

"Did Mrs. Price ever tell Mrs. Rudd that she had been threatened by her husband?" I asked.

"Not that I know of, but it was just his overall behavior. He was just mean. And then there was the New Year's party."

"What happened there?" George asked.

"It was quite the event with lots of guests. Most were people that Mr. Price did business with. The Rudd's were invited as well. In the middle of this party a man named Phineas Luck showed up. He had not been invited, but stormed into the house, confronted Allen Price and accused him of swindling him out of a lot of money. Allen Price did not back down and laughed at and made fun of Mr. Luck. Mr. Luck is a very small man. It was at this point that Mr. Luck said that he would get even with Price. He said some bad things were going to happen to Price and his family."

"Who heard all of this?" I said.

"I heard it from Mrs. Rudd who was barely ten feet away from the encounter and also from Martha, one of the maids the Prices used for the party. They both told me pretty much the same story."

"So Mrs. Rudd was a bit worried something bad was going to happen to Mrs. Price and several people heard this Luck fellow threaten Mr. Price?" I asked.

"That's about is, but the thing with this Mr. Luck was not that uncommon, Martha told me. Mr. Price had quite a few instances where people he was doing work for felt cheated."

We thanked Wilma for her time and the information and made our way to our vehicle. "What do you think, Moses?" George asked.

"We can toss the theory about Allen Price harming his wife out the window. He may have been a bastard, but that is not the case here."

"But Phineas Luck?"

"That's a different story. A visit to Price's office and a review of upset clients seems in order."

"Does someone shotgun and murder a whole family over the loss of some money?"

"It depends on how much money," I said.

• • •

Our questioning of other neighbors turned up little. We had expected to return to return to the precinct and prepare for our next venture which we thought would be a visit to Allen Price's former employer, Chicago Commodities. Instead, as soon as we walked into the building, we were told that a State Prosecutor was waiting for us in the first floor meeting room. The vehicle we had driven in had been beastly hot and Loftus and I looked like two wilted flowers. I doubted we'd make any positive impression on the lawyer who wanted to see us. This wasn't what bothered George.

"I've been up all day. I need a break."

"We'd better deal with this," I said.

The prosecutor looked like he was twelve or thirteen. He was a pudgy little thing with plump, rosy cheeks. His face had never seen or felt a razor. He was meticulously dressed in a navy, pinstripe suit, accompanied by an expertly knotted bow tie. I got the feeling he was late for his ninth grade English Literature class rather than being able to prosecute anything.

"My name is Jeremiah Higgins," he said. "I'm to be the lead prosecutor for the state against Madeline Marsden and Patricia Farmer."

Loftus, in a far than less professional manner, burst out laughing. "The state assigned you to prosecute those two murderers."

Mr. Higgins did not seem to mind the laughing or the question. "The state has."

"I think what Detective Loftus was alluding to was the fact that you don't look like you can be old enough to have gotten through law school," I said.

"Or high school," Loftus added.

Higgins smiled. "I may look young, detectives, but I did graduate and pass the bar. Northwestern Law, top ten percent. I have also prosecuted several recent cases. Doesn't matter. I'm here and you are stuck with me."

"Fine with us," I said. "Anyway, what is so difficult about this case? Those two girls killed the three women. This shouldn't be all that hard to try and convict."

"So you say," Higgins said, sifting through some papers. "Are you familiar with a lawyer by the name of Bradley Luke?"

I didn't think that George had met Luke, but I had. His assertion that Patricia Farmer was innocent of murder had sent me on my latest binge. "We've met."

"He has stated, obviously through his client, that Ms. Marsden did everything physical to the victims. She bound them to the chairs, she tied them up, she stuffed their mouths and she watched closely as they drew their last breaths. All sweet little innocent Patricia did was draw some unsettling pictures of the murder scenes. She was not a murderess. She was simply a bit of an unwitting accomplice. She was afraid of what the more physically equipped Marsden would do to her if she didn't accompany her or, Heaven forbid, say anything."

"That's preposterous," I said. "We heard that there was no doubt that Patricia was the ring leader. Madeline was a wallflower who got taken in by Patricia. What you're telling us is exactly opposite of what we discovered."

Lawyer Higgins shrugged. "That may be, Detective Moses, but that is what Mr. Luke is asserting. He's not a very charming fellow. I don't like him."

I hadn't either. "So what does this mean?"

"It means that you and Detective Loftus have to figure out a way to prove that Patricia Farmer is lying. You have to prove that this was her idea and that she coaxed your little wallflower, Ms. Marsden, into committing the murders. You have to prove that she was the dominant one behind all of this."

"That should be simple. All we need to do is talk to Madeline Marsden. We should be able to get the truth out of her."

"That is too simple. We have spoken to Ms. Marsden with her attorney present. Right now, believe it or not, she is insisting that it was all her idea, she did all of the dirty work and Patricia Farmer only tagged along and drew some pictures. In her own words…" Higgins shuffled more papers. " 'Patricia came with me. It was my idea. I did everything bad to those women. All Patty did was sit there and draw some pictures'."

"That's crazy," I shouted. "Why would she put herself out there like that and defend Patricia Farmer?"

Higgins snapped his file shut loudly. "I am only a humble prosecutor. It is you two detectives who must look into this and figure out what the hell is going on. If all holds as is, and we can try the girls as adults, Marsden could get the rope, but probably life. Patricia Farmer could get off with way less a sentence."

I had been coming to Coopers for many years. It wasn't odd that I came here more than once in a day. It was a quiet little place that did a modest business with a consistent following by the locals in the area. I found that it gave me time to think. I had known for a long time that I didn't come there for the food, which was never very good, or the beer, which was seldom the right temperature. I came there for the relative quiet even though it was located further from the apartment I was renting. I came there because it was the closest thing I had to a home.

This evening I had chosen a chicken with beans and boiled potatoes. Surprisingly the chicken was tender and tasty. The beer I had was a little warm and a bit watery. I thought of bourbon, but that thought dissipated as I thought of my last trek along Bed Bug Row. I figured staying with the watered down beer was a safer bet.

No sooner had I resolved that Coopers was not a place I could do without when I looked up from my plate of food into the rough looking face of Captain Jack Garfield. I hadn't seen him since we had arrested one of his detectives, Daniel Bergman, and charged him with extortion. He didn't look any happier to see me.

"Enjoying your dinner, Moses?"

"I was, Captain. Sit down and I'll buy you a beer. You can tell me why it is that you came to visit me."

Garfield looked a bit surprised, but pulled out the other chair and sat down at the table. He looked around the premises for a bit. "Nice place," he said.

"It's usually a quiet place. I have a feeling tonight won't be so quiet for me."

He smiled. The waitress came over, but Garfield waved her away. "I hear you were quite the guest while you stayed at The Bitter End."

Word had a way of travelling quickly and far in the Levee. "I offered to pay Mrs. Flint for any of the damage that I did. I have not heard from her with her accounting."

"Some broken mirrors, a cracked window, torn bedsheets and a dresser that looks like a hole has been kicked in it."

"You seem rather up to date on the damage I caused."

"Mrs. Flint and I have a relationship, a rather long one."

"I will pay her," I said.

"And the girls you hurt?"

Looking at Garfield he appeared very smug, like he knew something I didn't. "I was told that there was no injury to any of the girls."

"None that they may have told you about, but there were some. Brothels that rat out the police sometimes don't do well business wise for a while; sometimes they actually fail, but I really didn't come here to talk with you about a few banged up whores."

I found a bite of the chicken that was a little chewy, but the warm beer helped me get it down. "I didn't think so."

"Your landlord, or should I say ex-landlord, was shot in the head at close range with a medium caliber revolver. This happened the night before your neighbor, Mrs. Lois Winston, another murderer, went missing with her son. Don't you find that a bit odd, Moses?"

"The gun that Lois had was a .45. The hole in my landlord's head was not made with a .45. Most of his head was still intact. Lois did not kill him."

Garfield nodded. "Maybe not, but what about his murder and her leaving being connected? I just find this all very odd."

"I understand that somebody planted Mr. Winston in the garden of their old home. Must have been Lois because she left soon after the news broke. I don't think she killed the landlord on the way out the door."

"And no idea how Mrs. Winston learned about her husband being found and decided to take off?"

"None at all," I lied.

He nodded again. "Why is it Moses that mysterious shit seems to follow you around? The death of your father, the murder of Amos Stokes, with the same gun I say, and now this Lois Winston thing. You never seem to be very far from any of these cases."

"Bad relatives, bad husbands and bad neighbors, what can I say? I guess I'm not on the luckiest streak."

Garfield slammed his hand on the table, bouncing my plate into the air. "I don't find you funny, Moses. I think you know a lot about all three of these cases. I've said it before and I'll say it again. I think you're involved and I intend to find out. I think there is either evidence or witnesses that know what I want to hear. I will find them, Moses, and when I do I will prosecute with no hesitation."

With that, Garfield rose from his chair, nearly upending it, and strode from the restaurant. His little speech and ending explosion hadn't upset me at all. He'd never get me for shooting my father on Christmas day or killing the fat slob, wife beater, Amos Stokes. With Lois Winston, I hoped she was way out of town. She knew a lot about me, but I was pretty sure I knew a lot more about her. She was a shitty gardener for sure. She hadn't managed to bury her abusive husband William deep enough in the ground. This alone could top anything she had on me. I doubt she'd come back to Chicago and relay any of her hidden secrets. One thing was also for sure. I knew who had killed my landlord. Christian Hanson, in his bid to find me and kidnap Freddie Winston, had killed him, but I was going to keep that from Garfield. Hanson was my special project. I would deal with him on my own when the time came.

•   •   •

Sleep wasn't easy to come by that night. It had nothing to do with what Jack Garfield had said to me. I found myself staring at the ceiling in the dark of my room considering the two challenges that I faced. The murder of three older women by two teen aged girls seemed like a wrapped up affair. The murder of an entire family by a supposed would be robbers had no clues and many unanswered questions.

Lying in bed, I found my stomach tighten thinking about Madeline Marsden and Patricia Farmer. It was clear that both girls had been present in the apartments of the dead women. This new story that Patricia Farmer wasn't responsible for the murders was appalling. Equally bizarre was the story that Madeline Marsden was taking the blame for the whole thing. Even if it was true that Madeline had done all of the physical things, how could Patricia come off as anything, but complicit? I had met Attorney Luke and he seemed adamant that that Patricia was not guilty of murder. I wasn't a lawyer and really wasn't sure how a judge would look at it, but it was a confusing issue.

It was clear to me that neither George Loftus nor I could determine the law covering the case. What we could do was find out why Madeline seemed so intent on taking all the blame and letting Patricia get away with getting the lesser charge. That we could look into and provide some clarity on.

My newer case, the murder of the Price family looked on the surface to be a robbery gone badly. The house had been completely tossed, including pictures torn from the walls. Whoever had killed the family had obviously been looking for something. Whether they found it was another question.

Our discussions with the neighbors on either side of the Price house, determined that Allen Price had not been a very popular person. The story that Dorothy Carruthers told about the party and the intrusion of Phineas Luck was an interesting one. Again the question here was money. Had Mr. Luck lost enough money by dealing with Allen Price that he made the decision to murder a whole family? This was the first angle that we would pursue tomorrow as we visited Mr. Price's former employer, Chicago Commodities. Maybe we could learn something from this visit. Maybe not.

Day Two

Not only did my frequent thoughts keep me awake, but a pounding on my front door at two a.m. drove me out of bed, revolver in hand. Instead of opening the door cautiously, I flung it open, prepared to shoot whoever it was that was causing this ruckus.

George Loftus didn't seem too alarmed when he saw the gun in my hand. He did seem amused at my worn and somewhat tattered pajamas. "Get some adult clothes on, Moses," he said as he entered my apartment. "I have a car waiting. There has been a murder."

I lowered the gun and took in what George had said. "A murder? Who and where?"

"The corner of 31st and Dearborn is where. Who is another story, but I can tell you that it was a cop, a first year patrolmen. Don't even know his name."

I got dressed as quickly as I could and followed George downstairs to the auto he had secured. It was a short drive to the scene of the murder, just south of the Levee. There was a good sized crowd at the intersection. Most appeared to be with the police. When one of us gets shot, there is a common bonding, intent on killing whoever did the shooting.

We made our way through the crowd of mostly uniformed cops where we found Harold Pinter bent over the poor officer who had been shot dead. Like most of us, he looked like he had dressed quickly with little regard for appearance.

"Ah, Patrick," he said. "Hello, George."

"Good evening, Harold," I said. "What have you got for us today?"

He pointed at the uniformed figure lying on his back on the sidewalk. "This is, or was, I should say, Marvin Kell, a first year patrolman. He was probably doing his last round of the night when someone came up to him and fired one shot between his eyes. I would say that young Marvin may have known the shooter or at least wasn't alarmed by his approach. His gun is holstered and the holster is buttoned shut. It looks like Kell fell straight backward onto his back looking up at the sky as he is now."

I bent over and could see that Marvin Kell's eyes were wide open, staring up at the clear, summer night. There was a neat hole in the center of his forehead. "Obviously no clues?"

"None yet, but I'm certain I can find the bullet and do some lab tests on it," Harold said as his glasses slipped down on his nose.

"And nobody heard or saw anything?" George said, looking over the crowd.

"That's not exactly true. There's another patrolmen across the street. I told him to go there until the detectives showed up. He is holding a witness, I guess."

"A witness?" I said.

"You'd better go see what he has to say."

George and I made our way out of the onlookers and across the street where a huge cop was standing over a man who was sitting on the ground. For lack of a better word the man on the ground had the look of a vagrant.

"What have we got here?" I said.

The big cop pointed out the sitter. "Says he heard the gunshot and saw something, but I don't know. The guy stinks, smells like an alley mixed with bad booze, and what he is saying makes no sense at all."

"Can he stand?" George asked.

The cop lightly kicked the sitter in the bottom of his shoe. "Get up so the detectives can talk to you."

The man glared up at us. What light there was from street lamps showed the red in his eyes. He didn't look very capable of standing. I knelt beside him and the cop was right. The man stunk. "What's your name?" I said.

"McGuire," the man said clearly.

"Can you tell me what you heard or saw?"

McGuire looked straight at me. The red eyes made me wince. He also had some green stuff seeping from one eye. He was a sick drunk. "Heard a shot, loud, a big bang. There was no other noise tonight. Knew it was a gun. I looked over and saw a police van turning from the corner and going the other way. I walked over and seen that cop with the hole in his head. I just sat down there. I was tired."

I stood up. "Who called in the shooting," I asked the big cop.

"Came in from a call station. The response was quick and we found this fellow sitting by Officer Kell. He told us what he just said and the sergeant said to bring him over here until the detectives showed up. He hasn't said anything else."

I knelt back down. "McGuire, you see anybody near the body or getting into the police van?"

Again those red eyes gazed at me. I hope he lived long enough to give us some details. "No people," he said. I stood back up.

"Son of a bitch," George said. I knew what was bothering him. "If this drunk is right we have a cop shot dead in cold blood and a police van leaving the scene."

"This won't go over so well," I said.

"You don't think so?" George said.

I told the big cop to call for an ambulance to take McGuire over to Cook County Hospital. We walked back across the street to where the body of Officer Marvin Kell was being loaded into the coroner's van. This was a shitty start to what promised to be a long day.

•　　•　　•

After returning to my apartment for a few hours of marginal sleep, I arrived back at my desk around nine in the morning. We had called ahead the day before and had a scheduled meeting with Chicago Commodities at eleven; that would give Loftus and me a chance to review all three cases and decide what direction to go in next. This thought was short-lived. I was told that once Loftus showed up we were to report to Lieutenant Shipley's office.

Thankfully George showed up close to ten o'clock. With our planned meeting at eleven this would allow us to avoid a long altercation with Shipley, but there was plenty of time for the Lieutenant to get his points across, good or bad.

When we entered Shipley's office I could tell what kind of mood he was in. The tightness of his tie at his throat made it look like it was that that was causing the redness in his face. He was either very angry or stress was playing a toll on him. It could have been both.

"Captain Garfield gave me a summary of your antics at The Bitter End," Shipley said.

"Certainly biased. I don't think the captain likes me very much."

Shipley stretched his neck in both directions. "Moses, I think you are a good detective or you wouldn't be here. I find some of your methods distasteful, but your results are very good. I've warned you about Garfield. He does seem to have it in for you and I can only protect you so much."

I was going to say I didn't need protection, but Shipley seemed to be saying something nice. "I'm not trying to deliberately bother the captain."

Shipley smiled his usually weak smile. "The latest debacle is the murder of Officer Kell. What can you tell me?"

"Standing on the corner of 31st and Dearborn where he was apparently approached and shot once in the head," Loftus said.

"Witnesses?" Shipley asked.

"Not really a witness," I said. "A drunk heard the shot and started over to where Kell had fallen."

"But he saw nothing?"

"No. He saw a police van leaving the corner at a high speed."

Shipley shook his head. "This drunk heard the shot, starts across the street and sees one of our vans leaving the scene."

"That's what he said," I answered.

"How drunk was he?"

"Very, but he claimed he had a clear recollection of what he had seen."

Shipley closed his eyes and ran a hand through his graying hair. "This is problematic. I'm sure you can guess that I have already heard from headquarters."

"That is what we know so far. We haven't even gotten to where we've discussed our next move."

Shipley nodded. "The Price family?"

"Just starting there, too. Looks like a robbery; the whole house was tossed, but can't really tell," George said.

"The neighbors on both sides of the Price home told us that Mr. Price was a bit of a bastard," I said. "Said he wasn't nice to his wife, kids, employees or clients. Had a rather nasty row at a party he hosted with a former client. Again, we are just getting started. We'll see Price's employer at eleven to see what we can learn there."

"My god," Shipley said. "A whole family shot gunned to death, even the children. This is almost as bad as the Old Lady Murders."

"All murders are bad to me," I said. "I don't rate them."

"Speaking of that last nasty crime, the state attorney has told his boss, who told me, that Miss Farmer's attorney is going to be a bit of a problem. I heard this late yesterday."

"This is what I alluded to," I said. "I think this attorney, Luke, means to cause problems."

Shipley waved a hand at me. "I just want convictions for these girls."

George coughed loudly. "The problem seems to be whom did exactly what at each murder scene and should both girls be charged with murder."

"That's preposterous," Shipley said. "Both girls were present for the murders; don't they both get the murder one charge?"

"So we thought," I said. "The lawyer, a snaky fellow, contends his client did nothing physical to any of the victims, caused them no bodily harm at all. All she did was watch and draw some pictures. He claims that Madeline Marsden did all of the nasty stuff," I said.

Shipley sat back in his chair and rubbed his temples. "I want convictions for both girls. They both knew of and helped commit the murders."

"We thought so, too, but Lawyer Luke says no. The other part of this problem is that Madeline Marsden agrees with what the lawyer says. She's taking the blame for everything."

Shipley smiled again. "I seem to remember you telling me, Moses, that these charges would stick."

I felt my throat tighten. "I think the lawyer is nuts and I think these charges will stick."

Shipley pointed a long finger at me. "Proving that will be good for all of us, but especially good for you, Patrick. Raising your stock could prove valuable if Captain Garfield comes calling about you again."

Going down the stairs, Loftus grabbed my arm. "You seem to have a number of friends throughout this fine department."

"I don't like all of them, either."

"Just don't get me killed, Moses."

I smiled. "I never plan these things, George."

• • •

We were going to be late for our meeting with Chicago Commodities so we hustled down the stairs towards the exit near the desk the sergeant sat at to greet visitors. I happened to glance at the desk. Sergeant Cooley was on duty; standing in front of him was a middle aged woman and a very pregnant younger woman. Cooley waved his hand at me. "Moses, if you have one moment for these women."

I almost didn't stop moving, but my little hesitation gave the older woman plenty of time to turn from the desk and get right in front of me. She was a shorter woman with gray, curly hair. The clothes she wore weren't dirty but they were old and had seen a lot of use. Her eyes were bluish gray and were surrounded by skin tormented by wrinkles and lines. "You are Detective Moses?" she said loudly.

I looked at Cooley. He simply shrugged.

"I am," I said.

"I am Marvin Kell's mother. I want you to tell me right now what you are doing about my son's murder. The desk sergeant had no answers for my question."

Out of the corner of my eye I could see Cooley laughing. "I'm sorry, Mrs. Kell," I said dumbly. "We have just started the investigation and I'm afraid there is very little I can tell you at this time."

She put her hands on her hips and took a step towards me in a defiant pose. "You are going to tell me that my Marvin, a police officer, gets gunned down in the open and you can't tell me anything about the case?"

I looked over at Loftus, but he was looking to the side, wanting nothing to do with my little encounter. "Again, I am sorry, but there's not much I can tell you. What we do know is that Marvin was shot during his last rounds of his shift. We don't really have anything else at this moment to say." I left out the part about the police van.

Mrs. Kell looked down for a second and threw a thumb at the young, pregnant woman behind her. "And what am I to do with this one?"

The young woman blushed and lowered her eyes. "Who is she?" I asked, but I knew.

"This is Marvin's wife, Magda. Doesn't speak a word of the King's English and seven months pregnant, due in October. I didn't like her when Marvin brought her around and I really don't like her now. Marvin had to go get her pregnant, but at least he had the salary from the force. What the hell am I going to do now that Marvin is gone?"

I took the only shot I could. "There is no Mr. Kell?" I asked.

Her eyes bugged open. "That bastard took off years ago without a trace, so no, it's just me and Magda."

"We gotta go, Moses," George said quietly behind me.

Just then Riley O'Donnell came walking down the hall from the opposite side. In his one hand he was holding a rather large pastry. "Riley," I said. "We need your help."

Riley looked confused for a moment, but walked over. "What is it, Patrick?"

I pointed at the two women. "This is Marvin Kell's mother and wife. They need some guidance about what the department will do for them due to Kell's death. Maybe you can take them into a meeting room and find somebody who can help them out. Loftus and I have and urgent meeting we need to attend."

"But I've got a follow up to make on your landlord's murder and have some calls to make on Lois Winston. I'm up to my ass in calls."

I looked over at the two women. Mom was steaming inside; Magda still looked embarrassed. "Detective O'Donnell will take care of you and try and help you out with your questions." Before either lady or Riley could say another word I walked quickly past the women towards the exit; George, as if on cue, was fast on my heels. Riley may have shouted something after me, but his mouth was too full of pastry for me to understand.

• • •

The office for Chicago Commodities was located on LaSalle Street not too far from where my good friend Stanley Kerjewski had his law office. I hadn't seen Stanley since I'd uncovered a blackmail plot against him. I owed him a visit. Hopefully things were good.

Thomas Vance was the man we were directed to see. He had his office on the second floor and we were told that he that he had been Allen Price's direct boss. As expected, Vance's office was a lot of mahogany and leather, clearly first rate. Vance, on the other hand, didn't fit the décor. He was a big man and round. Whatever part you looked at there seemed to be fat spilling over. My guess is he weighed close to three hundred pounds. Every thread in the custom suit he wore was strained. He also had a full head of black hair and a mangy looking black beard that drooped well below his chin. I could tell he'd met with success in life and also that he didn't miss many meals.

"Gentlemen," he said to us as we took our seats across from his enormous desk. "Is there something I can offer you? Perhaps tea or a cup of coffee? It's a little too early for anything stronger." He laughed a bit.

"I think we are okay," I said. "We just wanted to ask you a few questions about Allen Price."

The little bit of joy he had on his face disappeared. "Terrible. Just terrible. Allen is one thing, but his poor wife and those children."

I looked over at George. "What do you mean by that?" Loftus asked.

I knew immediately that Vance hadn't meant this as any indictment. "I just couldn't believe the whole family had been murdered. It's bad enough one person gets killed, but four?"

"Let's return a minute to Allen Price," I said. "Tell me a little about him."

"Where to begin with Allen?" he said. "He was one of our top producers, an excellent broker. His specialty was agricultural products. Always on the top of his game."

"But what kind of person was he?" George asked.

"Do you mean is there any reason why you can see someone wanting to murder him?" Vance asked.

"That's what we mean," I said.

Vance first stroked his fluffy beard and then sat back and ran his hands over his enormous stomach. "Allen was a tough nut. He always seemed on edge, always looked like an animal stalking his prey. He was tough on his employees and tough on his customers as well. The only reason that customers stayed with him was because of his performance. He was extremely good at what he did. He was just irascible."

"So it is conceivable that he could have upset someone so badly that they took it out on him?" I asked.

Vance laughed again. "I don't know how often I had this vision of someone coming up here to the second floor and shooting Allen in his office. That seemed very possible to me."

"Allen fire any employees lately?" George asked.

"Absolutely not. As hard as he was on the people that worked for him they were loyal to him. He was successful and his group were rewarded handsomely because of his success."

"Angry clients?" I asked.

"There's always angry clients. There is always someone who thinks you didn't do well enough for them with their investment, but in Allen's case, it didn't happen often, again because of his success."

"Do you know a former investor of Allen's named Phineas Luck?"

Again the short laugh. "Everyone knows Phineas Luck. He invested with us and Allen for years. He did extremely well with his investments, mostly due to Allen. A while back there was a severe drought here in the Midwest. Allen had invested a good deal of Phineas' money in wheat futures. Allen and Phineas lost badly on that one I'm afraid. Phineas got very angry and threatened Allen on many occasions. Sometimes these threats were made publicly. Ironically, even with the wheat loss, Phineas made a large profit that year from Allen's guidance. Phineas didn't like losing at all."

"And he actually threatened Allen out loud?" George said.

"We were at the Union League Club and Phineas came up to Allen and challenged him to a duel, believe it or not. Allen just laughed at him. Phineas opened his jacket to reveal a holstered gun and said he ought to just shoot Allen now. Fortunately, cooler heads prevailed and Phineas left the club."

"Allen ever say anything to the police about this?" I asked.

"Never. He just thought that Phineas was an old wind bag."

"And what do you think?"

"Phineas Luck is an extremely wealthy man. Even with the loss in that one transaction he made money off of Allen. He was just irrational and maybe got tired of Allen being Allen. I don't think it was more than that."

"So you don't think Phineas Luck is capable of murder?"

"Detective Moses, Phineas Luck is a spoiled brat, big mouth. He's never had to work a day in his life. Nobody likes to lose money, but this gave Phineas the chance to bark at Allen a little. Remember this came after years of listening to Allen bray about his successes. Phineas is a big mouth, but he could never murder anyone."

"What do you think of Phineas Luck?" Loftus asked as we walked towards a call box on the corner.

"Well, he had the motive when Price lost him money, he owns a gun and he has a temper."

"We should probably pay him visit."

"Just because Thomas Vance says he wouldn't shoot somebody doesn't make it so."

"Shooting one guy that you're angry with and murdering an entire family are two distinct situations," Loftus said as he opened the box and lifted the receiver.

"That part is true. And who did Luck get to help him with that deed. It wasn't one man who killed that whole family. There's also the part about Price's home being torn apart. Why would Luck do that?

"The neighbor lady said it was a cover."

"And we thought the neighbor lady was a little addled."

Loftus shook his head and called into the precinct. I looked up and down the street at all of the business types who were strolling along LaSalle. This was the business capital of the city; the sidewalk was packed.

"We've got to get back over to the Levee," Loftus said, hanging up the phone. "They found an abandoned police van a couple of miles from where Marvin Kell was murdered."

•   •   •

The ride back to the Levee was quick and hot in the vehicle we had. The temperature was climbing every minute, the sun was glaring. I had a minute to think about what the police van meant. Had someone stolen it to use in the commission of the murder of Marvin Fell or was an officer involved? I didn't like either choice, but hated the second one.

The police van had been found near the Chicago Stock Yards, not far from Bubbly Creek where the dead body of my former love, Eleanor Winter, had been found on Christmas morning. The van had been driven into a stand of bushes and simply left there. Riley O'Donnell had been the first detective on the scene; Harold Pinter was with him.

"I'm not happy with you, Patrick," Riley said. "That woman was crazy."

"We had to go, Riley. I wouldn't have done it if we didn't have somewhere to be. I hope you were able to help the poor woman."

"I need help now," Riley said, "but I did find a name of someone at Central Station. I think she went in that direction."

"What have we got here?"

"This looks like the van your bum saw racing from the scene. It's from the 23rd. We could tell that, but not much else."

I walked past Riley where Harold was busy looking over the seats in the front of the vehicle. As usual he looked very intent. He thinning hair was matted down and his glasses were continually sliding down his nose. He looked up when he heard me approach. "Ah, Patrick. I'm glad to see you made it back before we had this brought in."

"Anything special you can tell me, Harold?"

"Nothing really. I'm sure there's finger prints here, but how many officers drove this van. There is absolutely nothing here that points me to who drove it here last night."

"You're pretty sure it was the van used last night?"

Harold righted his glasses. "No. Not at all, but it appears the killer drove away in a van. The next day a van is found stashed into these bushes. I'm not sure of this, but there is too much of a coincidence to pass it up."

I nodded. "No clothing, cigarette butts, blood, anything to help us out?"

"Not a thing."

I looked out towards Bubbly Creek, that small body of water that had once caught on fire. "You know, they found Eleanor right around here on Christmas."

"I know. That was only eight months ago. Seems like eight years. We get so many crimes down here and have so little manpower I forget about them, but some I remember. Some keep me up a night."

I wouldn't have thought the crimes got to Harold. He was always so focused I never saw emotion, but I never saw him after hours when you were alone with your thoughts.

"So what can you do?"

"Like, I said. Bring the van in where I can get a better look at it and maybe I can find something to help us, but I'm not hopeful."

I reached up to brush some sweat from my brow. Five murders in a couple of days and nothing to help us solve any of them. "You'll find something," I said. Maybe it was to encourage Harold, but it was more like me hoping out loud.

He smiled and straightened his glasses. "Maybe."

• • •

Patricia Farmer and Madeline Marsden were being held in the Cook County Home for Wayward Children. For lack of a better description it was a jail for children who had not reached the adult age who had committed a serious crime. The girls had not been arraigned yet as there was a lot going on regarding pleas. Right now it seemed like Madeline was trying to take the blame for just about everything while Patricia said she was only a tepid accomplice. This line was a serious problem for Madeline if the judge decided they were to be tried as adults, if a trial took place. Right now Patricia was in some trouble, but maybe not so bad. That was what we had to work out.

Sally Marsden and her husband Richard were at home when we called on them. It was actually Richard that spoke to us; Sally was still in shock from the whole affair and was taking up refuge in her bedroom under some sedation. We hadn't met Richard, but he seemed like a normal guy, tall, skinny and with a receding hairline. He wore a coat and tie, but I didn't think he'd be going anywhere that day.

"I'm sorry about Sally," he said. "She's just trying to understand all that's been happening. It's been very tough on her."

"I can't imagine," I said.

"She would love to participate, to help in any way she can. She is just not up to it," he said.

"We spoke to Madeline's lawyer. We told him what we were trying to figure out and he said the best place to start was with you and your wife before we went and saw Madeline. That's why we called."

He turned and stared out the window at the hot, sunny day that was taking place outside of his home. It was cooler inside, but not by much. "It's very hard as a parent to hear that your daughter has been arrested for something like this. To hear that your daughter is involved in murdering three elderly women is unimaginable. It was like a hard punch to the stomach. To then hear that she is taking sole responsibility for the murders is beyond reasonable thought. It is some kind of nightmare that just will not go away."

The conversation was clearly making Loftus nervous. He looked like he wanted to go outside for a smoke. I felt bad for Richard and his poor wife. I could clearly not imagine their pain.

"You know," Richard said, "I didn't think that Madeline was capable of hurting anything. She would get upset if I killed a bug in the house; she wanted me to catch them and put them outside. She loved all animals. We were at a farm once where a horse had to be put down. It was awful to see; Madeline cried the whole way home. She wasn't herself for a couple of days. That's why this is so out of character for her. Killing three women. That's not her."

"It's not like anyone," I said. "Tell me a little bit about what you know."

He ran his hand through his hair. "Sally thinks, and I have started to believe, that a change came over Madeline when she started to go around with Patricia. In some ways she was more confident, but there was something there. She always prefaced things by saying something like, 'this is the way Patty does it' or 'if I don't do this Patty will be upset.' It was very strange."

"How long have they been friends?" George asked.

"Towards the end of last school year and then into the summer. They spent a lot of time with the Daughters of the City."

"Did Madeline have a lot of friends before Patricia?" I asked.

"That's the other thing. Madeline was a bit of a loner. She was a great student, but she was quiet and really didn't have many friends. Patricia was the one friend that actually seemed close to her."

"Nothing else you can tell us?" I asked.

"Not really. You explain to me how a reserved, quiet child becomes a murderer. None of this makes any sense."

"We want to go in and talk with her. We want to see if we can figure out why she is taking the stand that she is."

Richard Marsden threw his hands up quickly. "By all means. At this point we need all the help we can get. If she maintains this story she could get the book thrown at her."

George and I nodded. He no doubt understood the ramifications of what his daughter was saying she had done. Again, I felt bad for him and there was a little flinch in my stomach. We had to figure this out.

• • •

Madeline Marsden was led into the room where Loftus and I waited for her. The home for children was not a prison so Madeline wasn't cuffed or anything like that. I was aware that some of the female guards would beat you if you got out of line. The one that accompanied Madeline was tall and thick. I didn't doubt that she could knock me out with a good punch. She pushed out a chair at the table and half pushed Madeline into it. Then she looked over at us. "Five minutes," she said. She left us alone.

Madeline was dressed in a bland, gray, baggy dress. Her curly hair looked a little dirty, some curls looked more like knots. She wore a forlorn look, not angry, sad. She wasn't looking at us.

"I'm Detective Moses. This is Detective Loftus. We were at your house when you were arrested," I said.

She raised her eyes towards me. "It was only a few days ago. My memory isn't that bad."

"Don't get smart," Loftus said. "We are here to try and help you."

She glanced at George. The look on her face was unmoved. "I didn't ask for any help."

"Look, Madeline," I said, "we've heard some things that you have said. Your parents, your lawyer and us are concerned about these comments. Some of the things that you have said can get you into real trouble."

"I haven't said anything that I don't mean."

I took a deep breath. Loftus lit a smoke. This girl was a tough one. "How old are you?" I asked.

Her eyes were down again. "I'll be fourteen in October."

"If somehow you are found to be guilty of three murders, either through a plea or a trial, you will spend the next four years here. Around your eighteenth birthday you will be transferred to the county jail where you will spend the remainder of your sentence, which could be life. If you make it until age seventy you could spend over fifty years in prison."

George blew out a large plume of smoke and laughed loudly. "She won't make age thirty in the county jail. Some of those women will eat her alive."

Madeline looked up at that comment. There was a little spark in her eyes.

"Come on, George. Don't frighten her," I said.

George waved his cigarette at me. "I heard of a young girl that went in there and after about a year they couldn't find her. No trace. She just disappeared."

"I heard that, too, but things are better now. That stuff doesn't happen that much anymore."

"But is does happen," Loftus said. "And some of those bitches will just kill you for looking at them wrong. And you know what? The guards don't give a shit."

"What do you two want?" Madeline said sharply.

"I want you to listen, Madeline," I said. "You telling anyone that will listen that you did all of the killing of those women while Patricia Farmer just sat there and drew pictures is going to get you the maximum sentence. Patricia will get sentenced as an accomplice, but her sentence will be much lighter. You'll eventually go to County for a long time. She could be out by the time she's an adult."

"I told the truth," she said. This time her comment was quieter.

"Think about it a while. We'll be back. You are in big trouble either way you go, but you'll be in less trouble if you tell the truth and help us. Patricia's lawyer is saying she did nothing, but watch and draw pictures. He claimed you are a cold blooded killer. Tell us the truth. Tell us what happened in those houses. If you can help us prove Patricia is lying and is just as responsible as you we might be able to get the state to go a little lightly on you." I let those comments sink in. Her eyes were down as she thought this over.

"Can I go now?" she said after a few moments. Before we could answer the door opened and the guard was there to get her. She got up and left quickly before she could say anything further to us.

"What the hell is going on here, Moses? Loftus asked. He looked perplexed.

I had nothing to say because I didn't know what to say. The situation with Madeline Marsden was very bizarre and very dangerous. For her.

•   •   •

It was a known fact that I spent too much time at Coopers eating my dinner. Many times I left the little restaurant under the influence of something. I would be an easy target for a killer who came looking for me. For some reason, this grim thought didn't sway my decision. I was eating dinner, more bland chicken and vegetables, when I felt a figure hovering over me. I didn't look up, not ready for another meeting with Captain Garfield.

"Join you?" a man's voice said. A man's voice that I recognized.

I looked up into the long face of George Loftus. He looked about as tired as I felt, but he wore a thin smile and he was carrying two glasses of whiskey. "Sure, Loftus. I could use some company."

He sat down and placed one of the glasses in front of me. "The bartender seemed to know what brand of bourbon you drank," he said.

"Probably guessed." I raised the glass and we toasted each other.

"I didn't mean to interrupt your dinner. I just had a couple of questions I wanted to run by you."

The whiskey burned a little going down. I had been trying to be good, but sometimes old friends brought back good memories. "You couldn't ask them while we were together all day?"

"Maybe not these questions."

I could see that George was serious. Something seemed to be bothering him. I pushed my plate away. "What's on your mind, George?"

Loftus sipped his whiskey and put the glass back on the table. "I was thinking about your partners, or I should say past partners."

"They were both good people," I said.

He nodded. "Sure. I don't mean anything like that."

"You mean how much did I have to do with them getting killed?"

"You know, Moses, rumors float all over the precinct. Sometimes they move all over the force. Word has it that signing on with you could get me killed."

There was something stuck in one of my teeth. I found it with my finger, a piece of chicken, and got it out. "I tend to end up with some lousy cases, chasing some bad people. At times there is violence. During some of those times people do get injured or killed."

"I get all of that, Moses. What about your partners?"

"Well, they both were killed by this animal, Christian Hanson. One went out looking for Hanson alone and ended up getting beaten to death; the other just wasn't lucky. He walked into a brothel room before me and nearly got his head blown off. Could have been me. He just went in first."

"This guy Hanson around town?"

I thought of Freddie Winston, naked by the pier by the river. "He's around. He and I don't care for each other. Something will give sooner or later and one of us will die."

I saw George's Adam's apple bob in his throat. "I meant either Hanson or me," I said.

He took another sip of his whiskey. "One more question, maybe it's two."

"That might cost you another whiskey."

He looked at my mostly full drink. "I've just got to ask this one."

Now I took my drink and took another sip. "Go ahead."

"There's a lot going around about the murder of your father and the murder of a guy named Amos Stokes. Quite a few people think that you had something to do with both of them ending up dead."

"You been talking with Captain Garfield?"

He waved his hand at me. "Not a chance. I've just got to know."

"What would you like to know?"

"Did you kill them, Moses?"

"My father was a crooked bag man for Aldermen Coughlin and Kenna. Amos Stokes was a wife beater. Death might have been too good for them."

"So you killed them?"

"What did you think, George?" I felt a big smile covering my face. "You think I killed them?"

George raised his glass and looked over the top of it, but it never got to his lips. "Don't get me wrong about this, Moses. It sounds like both of them deserved it. I wouldn't hold it against you if you did it."

"So what do you think?"

"Maybe the Stokes guy, but not your own father."

I took a drink. "Maybe we'll find out soon. Captain Garfield is on a mission to find the truth."

He nodded again, taking a drink. "The head of the 23rd and Phineas Luck in the morning tomorrow?"

"First thing," I said. "Then a visit to St. Regina. We've got to find out more about this relationship between Madeline Marsden and Patricia Farmer. Sister Margaret Mary should be able to help us out."

Loftus rose steadily from his chair, knocking back the rest of his whiskey. "Again, Moses, I didn't mean to disturb your dinner."

I watched him leave and took a sip of my own drink. It felt good now. I hadn't lied to George about anything and part of me felt like if I told him the whole truth it wouldn't have mattered. He was right to be concerned. My luck with partners hadn't been good. I had warned him about Hanson. He would pop up somewhere and there would be violence.

I was about to get up and leave, but the waitress stopped by with another whiskey. "From the friend you were with," she said. "Said you deserved it."

I laughed and got comfortable for a bit. Loftus was a good man.

Day Three

It was extremely hot and humid the next morning. Our short ride over to the 23rd Precinct, a little to the south of us, was uncomfortable and quiet. Loftus didn't bring up anything about last night's meeting so I didn't either. I figured the matter to be closed.

When we got to the 23rd we were led right into the small office of Captain Bill Callahan. Callahan had a solid reputation and was said to be a good guy to work for. He also had an old past of being a brawler and he looked it. He was well over six feet, wide in the shoulders and chest and sported a nice scar on his nose and one across the bottom of his chin.

"The whole damn thing has everyone in the precinct a little jittery. I mean this kid Kell was on the force for less than a year and gets shot at random while standing on a street corner. Unbelievable," Callahan said.

I leaned forward in my chair. "What makes you think it was random, Captain?"

Callahan looked at me sideways for a minute. "You think that someone had it in for Marvin Kell? What could Marvin Kell do to anyone in the time he was on the force to get himself shot in the head?"

"I don't know," I said. "That's why we are here."

"Look, I don't mean to snap at you boys, but Kell was a first year patrolman. He lived with his mama and his wife, his pregnant wife.

He was just some dumb old kid trying to get his life going. Some crazy person saw the chance to kill a cop and they did it."

"You are aware that a police van was taken from your lot last night, found this morning and that a van was spotted leaving the scene of the shooting right after it was committed?"

Callahan sat straight up in his chair. His neck muscles tensed. "I knew a van had been stolen and found. Nobody said anything to me about a van leaving the shooting scene."

"We didn't tell anyone until we told you. We were trying to keep it under wraps for a bit."

"But you're not insinuating that another cop is behind this shooting?" His broad face was reddening.

"I'm not insinuating anything. One witness heard the gunshot and looked across the street to see a police van turn the corner and drive away as fast as it could."

He seemed to relax a bit. "But you don't know that another officer was driving the van?"

"That we don't know. Our witness wasn't able to identify anyone." I left out the part about our witness being a drunk.

"There's a lot of cops here at the 23rd. I don't think I can ask them all if they had anything to do with the shooting of Officer Kell."

"But you can ask around a little. Discreetly. If a cop was involved in the shooting we certainly don't want that getting out either."

Callahan nodded. "I can ask around."

"We know he lived with his mother and his pregnant wife. Do you know much more about his private life?"

"Not much. I had almost nothing to do with the man, but he was a good worker, learning about the job. People said he was friendly. I heard he would finish his shifts and go right home to his wife. Why someone would kill this kid is a complete mystery to me."

"But you will ask around, see what you can find?"

"I'll ask around, but I'll stake my reputation that if a cop was involved it wasn't a cop from my precinct."

"Let's hope it's not a cop, regardless of where he came from."

Callahan looked confused for a minute. "Let's find out who did this to Marvin Kell."

"Think he wants to find that a cop from his precinct shot another cop from his precinct?" George asked on the way down the precinct's steps.

"He seemed a little concerned about things damaging his reputation."

"A little?"

"Let's hope he comes up with something. Right now we've got a dead patrolman with a crazy mother and a drunk for a witness. Not much there."

"Something will come up."

"You're optimistic."

"Well, I could say that we are totally fucked."

"Let's be optimistic."

• • • •

Phineas Luck was a small man. If he was over five feet tall I would have been surprised. We found him at home in his plush apartment, a view of Lake Michigan showing through the large front windows. He was smoking a small cigar which seemed to match his stature.

"We understand that you had a beef with Allen Price?" I said.

We were seated on a very nice couch in his living room. He stood as he addressed us. "I had quite a few beefs with Allen. Can you give me one in particular?"

George looked at his notes. "There was a party at Price's house where you confronted him in front of a crowd of guests; another time you showed up at the Union League Club brandishing a gun."

Luck smiled. "Brandishing might be a little bit of a play on words, an embellishment."

George wasn't smiling. "You showed up there with a gun."

"That is true. I did confront him at his home and at the Union League. I'm afraid that I do not have the best temper."

I watched him suck on the little cigar and flick an ash into a tray on a table. "We know there were disputes about money that Price lost while trading in commodities," I said.

He pointed the lit end of the cigar at me. "A lot of money, Detective. I'm not talking about money you lose in a poker game at the precinct."

"I don't play poker, Mr. Luck. We assume it was a nice sum of money and we assume it may have given you a motive to kill Mr. Price."

"Motive? Yes, there was motive. Allen had promised me this one wheat deal would make me a great deal of profit, but nature caused the deal to go south. I lost a lot. I was very unhappy, so I guess I had the motive. As much as I was angry with Allen and maybe I did want to shoot him, I didn't do it. I also don't think I'm remotely capable of killing his wife and his children. Frankly, I find it appalling that the police would find me to be a possible killer."

"Where were you the night that Allen Price and his family were murdered?" I asked.

"I was at a summer cottage that I own in Wisconsin. I was in the company of Ms. Sarah Brock. I can give you her contact information if you need it."

I was thinking that Ms. Sarah Brock would confirm what Luck was saying. "Who do you think might have murdered Price?" I asked.

"That's a good question. Allen had a way of making bold promises to attract investors. Maybe someone was not as civilized as I am. Maybe they lost a lot of money with Allen, lost their temper and paid him a visit. I'd review other Allen Price clients who have suffered a big loss."

I was thinking we could get that from Thomas Vance. "Anything else?"

Phineas Luck smiled broadly. "Your precinct is in the Levee?"

"In the heart of it," I said.

"Allen was a poor faro player who didn't like to pay his debts. Sometimes he would favor the ladies and forget to pay the madam. He seemed to think that his credit was unlimited and that it never had to be paid back. I would assume that this practice at the wrong brothel or faro parlor might get you in trouble."

Outside, George asked. "What do you think? Certainly a smart ass little fellow."

"That he was. We can ask Vance for more clients that might have lost money through investing with Price. We can also look into Price's gambling and other unpaid debts in the Levee."

"Patrick, don't forget that Luck didn't have to be the trigger man. More than one person did that killing. This guy has a lot of money. There are people who would kill for hire. You could probably pay them to tear up a home and make it look like a robbery."

I thought about that as we started towards St. Regina. "Thanks for cheering me up."

•　　•　　•

My good friend Sister Margaret Mary didn't look any more excited to see us as she had the last time. It probably didn't help that we had arrested two of her female students for the murders of three elderly women. There was also something that told me she didn't care that much for the police in general. The woman never smiled very much.

"I didn't expect to see you back here so soon, Detective Moses," she said. I was still surprised at how cool she looked dressed in her habit on a day in the nineties with matching humidity.

"I guess I didn't expect to be back here either."

"From what I've heard, Madeline and Patricia killed those women. There shouldn't be a lot more to the story."

I didn't want to get too far into the details of the case. "I'm looking for a little information about the relationship between the two girls."

"Their relationship?" She looked perplexed.

I was searching for the right way to phrase it. "I need to know a little about each girl from your perspective."

"Shouldn't be too hard. Madeline was a quiet girl, an introvert. She was never in any trouble, was a good student and, until now, I'd say you would almost not notice her."

"Many friends?" George asked?"

Sister Mary Margaret thought for a moment. "She was pleasant with everyone, but I couldn't put her with any groups of the girls. Like I said, she kept to herself."

"When did she and Patricia become friends?" I asked.

"It would have been towards the end of the last semester before we let out for summer. I noticed the two of them talking to each other. They seemed to have gotten very close. Then they both signed up for the Daughters of the City. They made sure they were together on every assignment and, well, you see where that got us."

"So they have only been friends for maybe a few months?" I said.

"At the most," she said. "Patricia transferred here after the holiday break. I'm not exactly sure when she started talking to Madeline."

"She transferred?" I asked.

"Maybe I should have mentioned this earlier, but she came to us from the public schools. When her parents came to see me about enrolling here, they said she had some kind of altercation at her old school and that a transfer would do her well."

"No idea what the altercation was?" George said.

Suddenly it felt even hotter in the small office. "I don't really know. Her grade reports showed her as a good student. It was later that I found she was an exceptional artist. I had no reason to suspect anything bad."

I nodded. "She had no problems with other students or the sisters here at St. Regina?"

"None. Very quiet and well behaved the first few months. It was like she discovered Madeline and picked her to be her friend."

I wondered if Patricia had somehow selected Madeline to be the right fit for what she had in mind.

"Can you give me a little idea about what is going on with these two? I don't really know Patricia, but I knew Madeline and I'm concerned for her," she said.

I was concerned, too. "Did you ever get the impression that Patricia was controlling Madeline?"

She laughed for the first time ever, a real laugh. "That is an understatement, Detective. There's no doubt that Patricia was the dominant one. Whenever you'd see the two of them walking about, Patricia was in the lead and Madeline was a good three to four feet behind. Several of the girls, after the arrests, said that Madeline would do whatever Patricia wanted her to do. A couple of the girls supposedly joked that Patricia got herself a new puppy."

George and I looked at each other. Neither one of us was smiling. I don't think we found it to be that funny.

Later in the day I wandered down to the little laboratory that Harold had in the basement of the building. His recent work of solving crimes in the precinct had gained him respect and Lieutenant Shipley had allowed him to take over more space for his testing and analysis. As usual, he was bent over a table, staring at something intently.

"Do you have a minute, Harold?" I asked.

He peeked up at me and slid his glasses back up on his nose. I noticed again how tired he was looking. "Sure, Patrick. Have a seat."

I took a seat across from him at the table he was sitting at. "Anything exciting?" I asked.

"I wouldn't say exciting. This is the bullet that was extracted from the head of Mr. Burkhart, your former landlord. A .38 caliber in not the best shape. Firing into a human skull will cause the bullet to flatten out and distort its appearance. The bullet is almost demolished."

"It did a pretty good job on Mr. Burkhart first," I said.

Harold smiled. He sat back in his chair. "Was something else on your mind today?"

"I guess the Price murders first and then Marvin Kell."

He took out a handkerchief and wiped his brow. It was hot on the lower level. There didn't seem to be any prisoners in the cells and I felt glad for that. "Really, I don't have much to tell you on either case. With the exception of Mrs. Price, the husband and two children were killed with a single blast to the head with a shotgun, close range, very messy. Mrs. Price was first shot in the back. She managed to crawl a little before someone fired two bullets into the back of her head. I don't have those bullets yet.

"As I told you originally, after we'd seen the house torn apart, there are probably plenty of fingerprints left by the perpetrators, but you'd have to catch someone before I could match one up with the other. This art has not been perfected, only used sparingly. It would be tough to get a conviction on that alone. Other than that I don't have much to tell you."

"And Marvin Kell?"

"No bullet back from the hospital yet. I'm not even sure of the caliber of weapon used, but the hole in his head seemed to indicate a .38 or larger."

"How about the police van?"

"That's interesting. Follow me."

He got up and led me across the room to another table. There was a microscope there. "Take a look."

I bent down and peered through the lens. What I saw was obviously a hair. A very dark hair. "A dark black hair," I said.

"Yes. Very dark black and very thick. Not human."

"Not human?"

"Probably from a wig. I found several of these near the driver's seat."

"You think our driver, maybe the killer was wearing a wig?"

"That's conjecture, Patrick. Non-human hairs found in the van suggests someone wearing a wig was in the vehicle and it may have been the driver. Whether that person was the killer is another story."

I nodded. "Again, it would probably help if I arrested someone."

He smiled. "That always helps."

"One more question."

His tired eyes told me he was exhausted, but he didn't say no. "Do you think it's possible for one person to totally dominate someone? I'm talking about someone having the ability to control someone else's actions."

"That's not my field, but in some of my reading, I have seen and heard of cases where one party was the controlling factor over another person. So much control in fact that they were able to manipulate the other person to do just about anything. Anything in particular?'

"I'm thinking that it might have been possible for Patricia Farmer to manipulate Madeline Marsden. I think she may have gotten Madeline to commit the worst part of the crimes while she never did any of the bodily harm to the women."

Harold raised his eyebrows. "You're a bringing me a number of examples of cases today that might be tough to prove in a court of law. Saying that someone talked you into committing a serious crime does not get you off the hook for actually committing the crime."

I saw where he was going with this. "I understand. It was just a theory."

He patted me on the shoulder. "I didn't say give up your thought process, but to prove something like that you'll need to be extremely clear and precise."

I got up to leave. I knew he was busy, but a thought crossed my mind. "Why don't you join me for dinner, Harold? It will be my pleasure to have you as my guest."

"That's very nice of you, Patrick, and a generous offer, but I have to stop and see my wife before heading home. I also have to get an early start in the morning."

I was confused. "I'm sorry. Where do you need to stop and see your wife?"

His eyes saddened. "I thought I had told you, Patrick. She is in the critical ward at Mercy. Cancer. They don't know how long, but they are fairly certain it will be shortly."

I'm sure I stood there for a moment with my mouth hanging open. I didn't have a clue about this. "I'm sorry, Harold. If there is ever anything I can do."

"I know, Patrick. I know."

•   •   •

Jim Colosimo sat across from us in his second floor office in Paris, the large brothel he owned on the north side of the Levee. It was said that "Big Jim" owned over twenty brothels in the district. As usual he was dressed in all white. His hair was excellently combed. Each finger on each hand was adorned with a gold ring. As cool as Jim looked, George and I were hot and sweaty. We had to take a horse drawn over to Paris and the ride had been pure misery after being able to use an auto the past few days.

"We are not friends, Moses," Colosimo said.

"What makes you think that I thought we were?"

"I don't want you thinking we are close because I knew your father or that Margaret Krause still makes dresses for my wife."

Hearing Gunter's ex-wife and my one time romance's name made me flinch. All of that seemed so long ago. "I don't assume that."

"Then why are you here? You're not here to ask me about Christian Hanson again?"

"I'm always looking for Hanson, but that is not the reason I'm here."

"I also see you brought a new partner with you," he said, pointing at George. "Partners don't seem to last a long time with you."

I didn't respond to that. "Do you happen to know the name, Allen Price?"

"Kind of hard not to. The *Tribune* has had his name all over its front page the last couple of days."

"Know or hear of him before that?"

Colosimo shrugged. "Should I?"

"A source we had said he liked to play faro here in the Levee. Liked the ladies and the booze, too."

A big smile. "Sounds like a lot of men in the Levee."

"Price was not a very good faro player. He'd lose a lot of the time and then not want to pay his debts. Also had a penchant for running up debts at the brothels and forgetting to pay them."

"Not at my places. You might forget to pay one time, but I've got people that will help you remember. You say this guy Price tried this stuff a lot?"

"We heard this was the way he operated if he lost."

"Sounds dangerous, but I've got to say I don't know any owners that would have somebody blow off your head for not paying. We also don't take out whole families and tear residences apart. Not just for forgetting to pay debts." He smiled again.

"Think you can ask around for me?"

He thought for a moment. "I don't like welchers, Moses. You come into my places and lose money or have a good time with one of the girls, you gotta pay up. That's all there is to it. So I give two shits about

Allen Price, but the wife and the two kids that hurts. I'll see what I can find out."

"Just maybe who he owed money to?"

"We'll see what we can do."

We got up to leave. "What was your name again?" he asked George.

"Detective Loftus," George said with a smirk.

"You watch that guy, Detective Loftus. One of his partners was beaten so bad they said he was spitting rib pieces out of his mouth. The other one still has parts of his brain on the second floor wall at The Last Dance. Don't be a fucking hero."

George swallowed hard. "I'll try and remember that."

"You do that and always have your gun ready and one in the chamber. There's always a shootout with Moses."

Hailing a carriage in front of Paris, I looked over at Loftus. He looked a little white. "Don't listen to that stuff, George. Colosimo just likes to puff out his chest and talk a big game."

He looked over at me. He wasn't smiling. "I believed what you told me about the bad luck and stupidity that got your partners killed. I also believed what he said about there always being gun play. Remember, I was there when we arrested Daniel Bergman."

For a second, I felt tense, but I relaxed. "I only shoot when I have to. It's not like I enjoy the chance at being shot back at."

George stared for a second and then nodded. The carriage had pulled up to get us.

•　•　•

I ate a gloomy dinner at Coopers, alone this time, with no visitors. I was feeling good when I stepped out into the warm night and hailed a cab to get me back to my apartment. I thought about the time that I got mugged in front of the place and Lois Winston had saved me by firing her .45 into the air. I also thought about what Colosimo had told George about having a bullet ready in the chamber. I felt for my gun in its holster and knew it was ready to shoot. I seldom worried about unwanted visitors, but at least this night I'd be ready if they came.

I had the carriage driver drop me off down the street from my building and walked the remainder of the way. As I approached my building I could see someone sitting on the steps. It was a woman. That didn't matter. No one ever sat on the steps. I drew my gun and slowly moved towards the building. I could see the woman better as I got closer. She was younger with dark hair. She stood up and I tensed. I felt a trap was near.

"Good evening, Detective Moses," she said.

I still had the gun in my hand. "Do I know you?"

"My name is Joan McDermott. I work over at The Bitter End. I knew Eleanor Winter a while ago."

This mentioning of my last girlfriend, murdered by an animal, still didn't relax me totally. My hand tightened on the gun grip. "And why are you sitting on the steps to my building, Joan McDermott?"

She looked down and noticed the gun for the first time. "I think you can put your gun away, detective. I am here as a friend. Eleanor always said what a decent person you were."

"I'll hold the gun for now. I haven't had the best of luck in front of this building before."

"I don't know what you mean by that, buy that's fine. I told you that I worked at The Bitter End. I was around when you paid your little visit not long ago."

"I wasn't mean to you or anything like that?"

"No. Not me, but I heard a couple of the girls say that maybe you weren't that nice of a guy."

"It wasn't such a great few days."

She laughed. "Anyway I came to see you because a Captain from the police has been coming around, asking questions about you. A Captain Garfield."

"I'm familiar with Captain Garfield."

"He'd definitely been drinking when he came into the house. He was yelling at the Mrs. Flint, wanting to know who had spent time with you during those couple of days. She wouldn't tell him and he became very angry. Said he had heard that you injured a couple of the girls. Said he was going to get the information one way or another. Then he stormed out."

"He doesn't care for me very much."

"I would say that he made that clear."

I laughed. "So you came all of the way out here to tell me that?"

"Like I said, I knew Eleanor and she said you were decent. I didn't want you getting in trouble with this Garfield fellow. I didn't like him very much."

I holstered my gun and stepped closer to her. Up close I could see she was young and pretty. On the right night I might have been tempted. We had an early start the next day. "I wish there was some way that I could repay you for helping me out by telling me this."

She gave me a smile. "You could invite me in."

I checked my watch. It wasn't that late and I hadn't been drinking. "That's the least I can do."

Day Four

The public school that Patricia Farmer had attended was the Abraham Lincoln School on the north side of the city. After finding a carriage and dropping Joan McDermott off, I made my way into the precinct where I met up with Loftus. George seemed in a particularly good mood, dressed smartly in a dark suit. We made our way to the vehicle in the back lot and began our trek to the other side of the city.

The principal of the school was a man named Clarence Feltes. We learned he would be in the school this morning getting ready for the fall semester to begin in a couple of weeks. He agreed to meet with us as soon as we could get there. It was not going to be a short ride.

"Do you think your friend, Mr. Colosimo, will come up with anything for us on the Price murders?" George asked.

I looked over at him. "I would hardly say we are friends, but I think he will try and help. In the back of my head, I think he will be looking for a favor from me one day. I kind of have this idea that it's a mutual thing."

"Maybe he can help. Right now, we need a break."

"I went a saw Harold yesterday in the afternoon. He's found something in the police van."

"A clue?"

"Maybe. A couple of medium length all black hairs."

"That could be something."

"Could be, but they are not human hairs. They appear to be from a wig."

"So whoever hit Marvin Kell was disguised, wearing a black wig?"

"That is a theory."

"We need a little more than fucking theories."

Maybe my thought that Loftus was in a good mood was wrong. We rode the rest of the way to our meeting in silence.

•   •   •

Clarence Feltes was an odd looking man. He had a particularly small body and a neck and head that didn't seem to fit it. On top of that he wore thick glasses and his hair was growing only around his ears. He peered anxiously at us as we met with him in his office.

"I was hoping that I would never hear the name Patricia Farmer again, but I was not surprised when you called and said you wanted to speak about her."

He was staring intently at us; it was hard to make out his eyeballs through the thick lens. "I take it that your experience with her was not that wonderful," I said.

"Detective Moses," he said loudly. "Little Miss Farmer is as close to the devil as you can get. My experience with her was as close to hell as I wish to get."

"How long did Patricia attend your school?"

"Just the fall of last year until she transferred out this year. Her family had moved here from St. Louis."

"So she was here for less than one year?" George said.

Feltes was nodding his big head. "That's it. Came in around September, left shortly after the holidays."

"I assume there was a significant reason for her departure?" I asked.

"If the families involved hadn't all reached some form of agreement, I was sure that I was going to have to call the police and report what I knew. As it was, all three families sat down with their attorneys and worked out a deal. Part of the deal was that Miss Farmer and Mr. Albright would transfer out of the school. I think their parents thought that was the best deal and they complied."

"Do you mind giving us the full story?" George asked.

He smiled lightly. "I've got time. It won't take that long and if it helps some way to lock up Patricia Farmer for a while, I'll be glad to be of assistance."

Feltes took a deep breath. "There was a boy in Patricia Farmer's class by the name of Timothy James. He is a nice boy, but not very popular. He is a bit slow."

I shifted on my seat. The early description was already making me uncomfortable.

"Mr. James took a liking to Patricia Farmer," Feltes continued. "I'm not really sure of all the details, but he was sweet on her. In my estimation, he may have been bothering her, trying to get her to like him and maybe be his girlfriend. You know, the typical adolescent behavior."

"I was raised and schooled in an orphanage," I said. "I missed out on some of the normal adolescent things."

Feltes gave me a funny look. "Let's just say that it appears that Timothy James was pestering Patricia Farmer. This is where Brian Albright enters the picture. Up until a certain point, Mr. Albright had no interest in Patricia. Absolutely none."

"But something changed?" George said.

"Yes. That something was Patricia Farmers' pursuit of him. She went after Brian relentlessly, I am told."

"Tell me a little about the Albright kid," I said.

"Big kid, not overly smart. Likes to participate in athletic endeavors. That seems to be his primary interest, until Patricia pursues him."

"And she was aggressive?"

"Very much so. She fawned over Brian. I understand that she may have been even a bit promiscuous. She got her hooks into him real deep."

"Wait a minute," George said. "Weren't these kids thirteen or fourteen?"

"You seemed surprised, Detective Loftus. Children began to do some interesting things when they hit their teens. They began to discover members of the opposite sex. You should know that."

"Detective Loftus is a slow learner in some aspects," I said, smiling at George. He gave me a hidden hand salute that said he wasn't happy with my comment. "So Patricia comes onto Brian?"

"That's correct. She does her best to corral him and she persuades him that Timothy James is pestering her."

"I take it that Timothy James is not a very big kid?" I asked.

"Not at all. A little short and a bit frail. And maybe with that you can see where this is going. At first Brian tries to intimidate Timothy, lightly threatening him, constantly embarrassing him. It got pretty bad. Like I said, Timothy was a little behind the rest of the children so he didn't catch on right away. He kept trying to pursue Patricia."

"So what happened?" I said.

"One day right after school, Brian went after Timothy as he walked home. He taunted and pushed Timothy. He told him to leave Patricia alone. Timothy wanted nothing to do with this. He kept trying to avoid Brian, to walk home. He never even responded verbally. This really set Brian off."

"And what happened."

"He beat Timothy up. Punched him twice in the face, breaking his nose. When Timothy went down on the ground he kicked him repeatedly. He broke some ribs. It was a sad encounter."

"People saw this?" I asked.

"At least twenty kids."

I was stunned. "Wait a minute. This Brian kid beats up Timothy, giving him two severe injuries and the police were not called in?"

Feltes shrugged. "It's very strange story. Mr. Farmer and Mrs. Albright teamed up and convinced the James' family not to press charges. It was not disclosed, but I think there was a monetary settlement. The James are not very affluent so any money was welcome. I guess the way they looked at it was that Timothy was hurt, but he would survive."

"What was your reaction?" George asked.

Feltes threw his hands up. "I was mortified. This is a public school but actions like that are in no way acceptable. I called in the Farmers and Albrights. They told me an agreement had been made with the James. I said that was fine regarding criminal actions, but as the head of the school I gave them two options. They could transfer out or I could expel Brian and Patricia."

I thought of our case. "How was Patricia during all of this?"

"How was she? She said she had no idea what Brian was going to do. She said he did it on his own to attract her attention. She claimed total innocence regarding the act."

"And Brian's story?"

"Disgusting really. He claims that Patricia bribed him with promises if he would get Timothy to leave her alone."

"Promises of what?" George said.

"Well, according to Brian, it was promises of sex."

George shook his head and wrote down some notes.

"Any witnesses to these promises?" I asked.

"Not relating to the promises, but several people overheard Patricia telling Brian that he had to take care of Timothy that day or she would stop seeing him. That was the day of the attack."

"And you believe Brian?"

"Undoubtedly. There's no doubt in my mind that she orchestrated the whole thing."

"Any idea why the Farmer family moved here from St. Louis?" I said.

"Not really, but I heard there were problems."

"Do you have an address for Brian Albright?"

"I can get you that. I heard he is doing well so the family might not let you speak with him, but you can try. Another thing. Watch out for Joe Farmer, Patricia's father. He is a loud, repugnant type. He is also very successful. I got the impression that he would do whatever he could to protect his daughter, even if she was totally in the wrong."

We had met Joe Farmer. From hearing Feltes' story and from my encounters with Patricia's new lawyer, Bradley Luke, it seems Joe didn't mind spending money on lawyers to get Patricia out of trouble.

"I really do believe that Patricia Farmer is an evil person. She seems to have a way of getting people to do things for her. She is very persuasive. I hope you can put a stop to her," Feltes said.

George and I exchanged looks. That was our plan.

•   •   •

Feltes gave us the last known address for Brian Albright. He also gave us the last school that Patricia Farmer had attended while she lived in St. Louis. The address for the Albrights was close by; it would be easy to stop there. As far as going to or getting ahold of someone in St. Louis, we'd have to see if we needed that. The address for the Albrights showed a small bungalow with an unkempt lawn. The August heat had beat upon it enough to make it look like a burned out dirt lot.

We pounded on the front door a couple of times and were about to give up when it was opened by a big kid in very good, athletic shape. Brian Albright was pushing six feet and was beginning to fill out. It looked to me like he was going to be much taller as he got older. Brian had a mix of blonde and brown hair that was uncombed at the moment. He didn't look wide awake and it looked like we might have woke him up.

"Can I help you?" he said.

Loftus and I flashed our badges and his eyes popped open at the sight of that. At least we had his attention. "You Brian Albright?" Loftus asked.

"Yeah," he said. "What did I do?"

"Nothing, Brian," I said. "We just want to talk with you."

"Is this about what happened at school? I thought that was over."

"It is," I said trying to calm him. "We just want to ask a few questions about what happened. That's it. Your mother around?"

He shook his head. "She works down in the loop."

"How about your father?"

He laughed. "I saw him once when I was about four. If you see him tell him I want to talk to him."

"I understand that part," I said. "Can we come in for a few minutes?"

He opened the door wider and we walked into the house and out of the heat. The house looked like it was in need of repair and much of the furniture we could see was old and worn out.

"Just you and your mom?" I asked.

"That's it. My mom works six days a week. I work early in the mornings with dairy deliveries. I got home just a while ago and was napping."

"Heard you were a pretty good athlete," George said. "Still playing?"

"Not this season. I work to pay for my schooling. Mom works to pay the bills and to pay for the settlement."

"For when you beat up Timothy James?" I asked.

His eyes dropped to the floor. "She'll probably be paying that for a long time."

"So why did you beat him up. We understand that he was a lot smaller than you."

"I promised a friend I would get him to stop pestering her."

"Patricia Farmer?"

"Yeah, that's her."

"So you promised Patricia that you would get Timothy to leave her alone. What did she promise you?"

His face blushed. "She said she would be my special girl."

"What does that mean?" George asked.

"You guys know. She said we could do things if I took care of this for her."

I nodded that we indeed knew. "She ever let you do anything with her before your beat up Timothy? She ever let you touch her or kiss her?" I asked.

He shook his head. "Nothing. It was all promises until I did it for her."

"What happened after you beat up Timothy?"

He laughed a little. "She stopped talking to me. Wouldn't even be seen with me. It didn't last long because Timothy's parents came to the school and complained. I was the one who beat up Timothy, but a number of people heard Patricia talking about it. She got dragged in, too. Her dad got a lawyer, a real pale looking guy, to work with Timothy's parents. He worked out how much money we would pay the James' family and that we would transfer out of school. In exchange for that, Timothy's parents agreed not to go to the police."

I knew who the pale lawyer was. "Patricia hasn't spoken to you since then?" I said.

"Not one word."

I felt bad for the kid. "She totally used you?"

He nodded sheepishly. "I believed her. I thought that she really liked me. She made me a promise after I agreed to do what she wanted. I guess I fell for her. All she wanted was someone to beat up this kid she said was bothering her. Afterwards, I heard that all Timothy ever tried to do was to be nice to her. When it was all over, I felt real bad. I had hurt Timothy pretty good. He had never done anything to me. I did that to him because I got fooled and lied to."

"You apologize to Timothy?" George asked.

"Not yet," Brian Albright said.

"Since you're not busy playing ball and have some time, it might be nice if you did that," George said. "Might do you a little good."

$$\bullet \quad \bullet \quad \bullet$$

"What do you think of Patricia Farmer now?" I asked on the ride back to the precinct.

George lit a cigarette and took a drag. "She is definitely a young lady who goes to great lengths to get others to do things for her."

"So far we have two victims, Madeline Marsden and Brian Albright."

"Wonder what the hell she did in St. Louis."

My earlier thought that we wouldn't need to look into her behavior there evaporated. I could see a pattern for her developing.

"That girl is a scary one, Patrick. I think she might be a real crack pot."

•   •   •   •

I still had Loftus' use of the words "crack pot" in my head when we got back to the precinct. Sergeant Cooley was at the desk and said there was a message from Jim Colosimo that had been placed on my desk upstairs. He also informed us that we had a guest waiting for us in the meeting room on the first floor.

We crossed the hall to the meeting room and opened the door. When I saw who it was the term crack pot came back to me. Sitting there at the table and looking extremely upset was the mother of Marvin Kell.

"Mrs. Kell," I said as we entered the room. I closed the door behind us.

"I have been waiting here for over an hour," she said.

"I'm sorry you had to wait, but we were out on another call."

"A call that was more important than the shooting of my son, Marvin?"

I took a seat across from her; Loftus stood off near the corner of the room and lit a cigarette. Mrs. Kell looked tired. There were dark circles under her eyes. "There's nothing that is more important than your son, Mrs. Kell."

"You have nothing new to tell me about his murder?"

"At the moment, no. We have been trying to find out if Marvin was having any kind of beef with anyone. Maybe there's something that led to him being shot."

"You mean like someone trying to steal his wife?"

I heard Loftus grunt, but I could see be the look on her face that she was serious. "What are you talking about?"

"It's Frederick Munch. He is the man who shot Marvin. He has been trying to steal Marvin's Magda for some time. He is the man who killed my son."

I took a deep breath. "Tell me about Frederick Munch?"

"What's there to tell? He works in the lumber yards east of Halsted at 43rd. He is a very big man with a bushy beard."

"What makes you think that he killed Marvin and wants to steal his wife?"

"Magda had seen Frederick Munch for a while before she met my Marvin. Marvin told me a little about him. They had some words when Marvin first started seeing Magda. Nothing physical as far as I know, but Marvin wouldn't worry me with something like that if it did occur. From what I know, Magda chose Marvin because he seemed to have a better future than Frederick Munch."

Loftus stepped forward and crumpled his cigarette in a tray on the table. "This talk is all very interesting, Mrs. Kell, but once again, what makes you think he killed Marvin?"

"Two things, Detective Loftus," she said coolly. "Frederick Munch has what you police call motive. Secondly, two days after Marvin was gunned down Frederick Munch came by my house with a carriage and Magda left with him. She has moved into his apartment near the stockyards."

I could see Loftus' eyes light up. "What do you think, George?"

He looked over at me and could see that I was smiling. "We'll take a look, Mrs. Kell," he said.

"You could also say thank you to me for helping you do your job." She was not smiling.

George's tongue seemed stuck. "Thank you, Mrs. Kell," I said. "We will pay Frederick Munch a visit."

•　　•　　•

Walking up the stairs to the second floor, George seemed to catch himself. "So now we have Frederick Munch the killer and wife stealer?"

"Worth a look," I said, "but I'm having trouble seeing a lumber yard worker disguise himself wearing a wig and then stealing a police van."

"That part bothers me."

"Better give it a look; though, or Mrs. Kell will be back here."

"She scare you a little bit, Patrick?'

"I don't know, George. She seemed to have you backing up in there."

He laughed. "She did at that."

The message that had been written down from the call from Colosimo was under a stack of files under on my desk. "Check with Eddie Gleason at Fast Times." That was all it said. Fast Times was a gambling parlor on Wabash.

"So what takes precedence?" George asked. "The murder of a cop or the murder of a prominent businessman and his family."

"Munch is probably at work in the yards. I say we head over to Fast Times to see Mr. Gleason. It's close and we can catch up with Munch later."

"Fuck, I'm tired," George said.

"Not much sleep last night?"

"How the hell can you sleep with all of the death around us and so little time and help to figure out what's going on? It's maddening."

Maybe my little fling with Miss McDermott had helped me sleep, but George had a good question and I had no answer. The whole thing with solving crimes was maddening. There were a lot of cases with little help. It could bring demons in your sleep.

•   •   •

We decided to walk over to Fast Times on Wabash to visit with Eddie Gleason. What I knew about Fast Times was that it was a gambling parlor with a couple of rooms upstairs for special guests. I had never been in the place, but I could picture how it looked before we walked through the door.

The place, like so many in the Levee had a long bar that was surrounded by tables meant for cards and dice games. At this time of day there was no one in the place except a fat bartender who was sweeping up in front of the bar. He wore a white shirt with a red bow tie. His pants were covered by a white, stained apron. On his head he wore a visor.

"Looking for Eddie Gleason," I said.

He looked up and me and went back to sweeping the floor. I thought he might have had a hearing problem. "I said I was looking for Eddie Gleason."

He looked at us again. "I made my payment at Alderman Coughlin's office. You guys don't have any beef with me."

"We're not here about any payoff," George said. He reached across and grabbed the broom from the man's hand. "You Gleason?"

"At your service," he said. He looked at me. "I knew your father."

I had no idea how he knew me, but I didn't care that he knew my father. "That doesn't endear me to you."

He shrugged. "Word on the street says you might have shot him dead."

"It also says I might not have."

He smiled now. "What can I do for you fine officers today?"

"Allen Price," I said.

"Now, there is a son of a bitch. Owes the club, me, about four hundred and he gets himself murdered. How the hell do you collect from the dead?"

"Doesn't sound like you made the best business deal spotting him that kind of money," I said.

"Doesn't take a Chicago detective to figure that out."

"Then why?"

Gleason rubbed his hands on the soiled apron. "Price was always in here playing and always losing. He was good for the house. I would let him play, he would lose, I'd give him some credit and he'd pay it back. This time I don't think I'm getting paid back."

"Don't think so. So he owed you a lot of money?"

"Whoa!" he said. "Don't go getting the wrong idea. I gave him credit and he always paid up. This time I lost out, but I had no reason to murder him."

"Not even if you thought he had the money in his house?" George asked.

"Look, why would I kill him. He'd have been here that night if he hadn't been killed. There's no doubt about it. He would have paid all or most of the debt off."

"Okay," I said. "You didn't kill him. Any idea who might have?"

"Specifically no, but he wasn't the nicest guy. When he lost at faro, which was a lot, he would yell at the dealers. He'd accuse them of giving him bad cards. If I let him go upstairs, he wasn't nice to the ladies, but he was just a pompous ass. He never got physical with anyone. The only one around here that he was always nice to was me. If he made me mad there was a good chance that I would not let him back in."

"That's a good reason which leads me to my next question. Why did he gamble here? No offense, but there are nicer places to lose your money," I said.

"No offense taken, Detective. From what I know, Allen Price had played in a lot of places and been banned from a lot of places. Come to think of it, he started playing here last year after getting into a big fight over at the Everleigh Club. Caused a couple of dealers to lose their jobs there."

"You don't say?' George said.

I wondered silently if all crimes in the Levee had a road that led to the Everleigh sisters and their club on Dearborn.

"If you need to you can talk to…"

"I know who to talk with Eddie," I said. "Any idea what the fight was about?"

"Yeah. Price was losing bad and accused two dealers of cheating him. The sisters didn't want the bad publicity so they fired the dealers. They also told Price not to come back. He ended up here."

"When was this?" George asked.

"End of last year."

We were walking back to the precinct in the Godforsaken heat. The Levee had that rotten, humid smell to it. I wondered if it ever went away.

"That Everleigh Club angle could have some legs to it," George said.

"Two dealers getting fired because of a complaint from a losing rich guy. They might be a little upset with Price."

"For some reason, I'm thinking you're looking at a different reason."

"I know Price made a lot of money, but I wonder sometimes if he could dip into his client's investment deposits and borrow a little to use at the faro table. With his losing habits he might have had a need to."

George stopped, lifted his hat and wiped his brow. "You think things like that are possible in a good firm like Chicago Commodities?"

"Guess we'd better go ask Thomas Vance a few more questions."

•   •   •

We made the mistake of stopping by the precinct before we headed over to see Frederick Munch. Munch would have still been working so we'd have been standing around anyway. As it was, we got back to the building and Sergeant Cooley informed us the Lieutenant Shipley wanted to see us as soon as we got back.

"Sorry Moses, but no more love notes or visits from Mrs. Kell," Cooley said. He looked ready to laugh.

"You could've just told her we were out for a while, Cooley."

"Sergeant Cooley, Moses. As for your advice, I told her you were out and didn't know when you'd be back. She said she would wait. I believe the Lieutenant is waiting for you two."

Rather than tell Cooley what I thought of him we headed upstairs. The door to Shipley's office was open and as we walked in he was popping two pills out of a little green jar.

"Not misbehaving, are we Lieutenant?"

Shipley gave me a dirty look and put the jar in his desk. "Bromide for my stomach. I wouldn't need it if people around here would do their jobs or at least keep me apprised of what is going on with cases."

We took the two seats across from him. "Where would you like us to start?" I asked.

Shipley emitted a fairly loud belch and looked embarrassed.

"Do you need a doctor?" Loftus asked.

He burped again, but covered this one with his hand. "The Price murders. City hall is beside itself on this one. Allen Price was a model citizen, donating to all of the proper causes. Getting his whole family murdered in a good neighborhood is not supposed to happen in our fine city. What can you tell me?"

"What I can tell you so far is that Price may not have been a model citizen. I won't deny that publicly he may have been a great person, but privately there was a different side to him."

The look on Shipley's face indicated his stomach didn't care for what I said. "Elaborate."

"He was a hard person to work with, both as a client and an employer. He got into it with one client over a losing investment case. The client allegedly threatened him with a gun. Really nothing there as the client was out of town when Price was murdered."

"Any angry or disgruntled employees?"

"None that we know of. He was hard to work for, but generous to the people who did. Nothing like that has popped up."

"What can you tell me that is promising?"

"George?" I said.

"Price likes to play faro and he plays badly. When he died he owed Fast Times around four hundred. The owner there said he was always behind, but always paid up. They liked him coming in there and losing, because he came back and lost more. They had no reason to kill him."

"That tells me nothing," Shipley said. He hand both hands holding his stomach as he sat back.

"Before Fast Times," I said, "he used to play at the Everleigh Club. Word has it that he accused two dealers of cheating him. He caused a big ruckus and they were fired. The sisters also asked that Mr. Price take his faro game elsewhere. He obliged and moved to Fast Times."

"When did the incident with the dealers occur?"

"End of last year. We're headed to see the Everleigh sisters as soon as we can. That is our best lead." Neither George nor I mentioned the thought about the possibility of Price using investor money to gamble.

Shipley nodded. "What about the murder of Officer Kell? I have had headquarters, the two aldermen and Mrs. Kell complaining to me. How could one of our officers be shot dead and nobody saw anything?"

"It was rather late in the day when most people are sleeping," George said.

Shipley looked again like he might be ready to blow up, but the belch passed. "What can you tell me?"

"Looks like the killer used a stolen van from the 23rd. Harold found some long black hairs in the van that appear to have come from a wig," I said.

"You think the killer wore a wig?"

"That's the one theory that we have. We also have news from Mrs. Kell that Kell's wife seems to have already moved on and is taking up residence with a man named Frederick Munch. We are going to try and see Munch this afternoon when he gets off work. He works out at the lumber yards."

"How much faith do you put in this line of thinking, Moses?"

"We won't know until we talk with Munch. Mrs. Kell says Marvin, her son, somehow got the wife away from Munch. Munch seems to be repaying the favor according to Mrs. Kell."

"So he shoots Kell in the head so he can steal the wife back?"

"If Munch is the killer that would seem to be the case."

Shipley suddenly put his hands over his face and then ran them through his hair. "Why do the cases down here always seem so convoluted? Can't there ever be any cases that we can clear easily?"

"What fun would that be?" I asked.

This drew a dirty look. "Onto the most bizarre. What of our two old lady killers?"

"Right now, Madeline Marsden is still taking responsibility for all of the murders. Patricia Farmer's attorney said all she did was sit there and draw pictures. She did none of the actual killing. According to the prosecutor, this may draw Madeline a very harsh sentence and Patricia a much lighter one."

"And what is the issue with that? I'm of the opinion now to just get the girls locked up and the case closed."

"That's fine, but we seem to be finding that Patricia Farmer is a master manipulator. It seems she has a history of getting people to do things for her and then slinking off with little or no repercussions. We've confirmed at least one more case of this."

Shipley stretched his this neck against his tight shirt. "Fine, but a conviction is a conviction."

"I don't see it that way, Lieutenant. I'm thinking that somehow Patricia got Madeline to be her friend and convinced her to do the killing part. Madeline was this quiet kid with no friends. Suddenly she's tied to the hip of Patricia. We think she told Madeline they could be friends as long as she did what Patricia wanted her to do."

Shipley closed his eyes for a moment. "But conviction or at least guilt is in line for both girls?"

"Looks that way, but I want the murder charge for both of them, first degree. I don't want Madeline to catch the brunt of all of this and Patricia gets a much lighter sentence."

"I'll leave that to the two of you. Those girls are behind bars and how the judge sees it may be out of our hands. With Allen Price, his poor family, and Marvin Kell, there are murderers in our midst and that is all I hear about every day. I know we are short staffed and I am sorry, but we need results. We need to clear these cases. Use every resource that you have to find these killers. Get over to the Everleigh Club and talk with the sisters. You have a relationship with them, Moses. Get over and see this Munch fellow. Clear these damn cases so we can get a little back to normal."

"Normal, Lieutenant?" I said. "What is normal down here?"

Shipley sat back in his chair with his hands resting on his stomach. He looked to be in physical distress. This was our sign that the meeting was over.

• • •

When I first saw Frederick Munch the theory about him being a killer who wore a wig seemed remote. Munch was a big, barrel chested man. He was thick in the arms and legs. He also had a full blonde beard and mid- length blonde hair that hung loosely on his shoulders. For some reason, he didn't seemed surprised that we had shown up at his apartment. He smiled at us warmly and invited us in.

The apartment wasn't more than one large room. The bed and a table were crammed into one side; on the other was a kitchen area with a small table and two chairs. At this table sat the pregnant Magda Kell. She looked to be eating soup out of a large bowl.

"You are probably here to talk about the murder of Marvin Kell," Munch said. He had an accent that sounded German

"Why would we be here to ask about the murder?" I asked.

He stroked his big beard. "I'm sure that Mrs. Kell told you that Marvin and I had several talks. They were not always pleasant."

"We got the impression that you felt that Marvin might have stolen Magda from you."

Munch looked over at Magda who was still eating the soup. I was pretty sure she didn't understand a word we were saying. "Magda and I were seeing each other. Marvin Kell meets her and promises that he can give her a better future, a better home. You can see that my apartment is very small. Mrs. Kell's house is bigger. Marvin and Magda get married and she moves in over there."

"She didn't love Marvin?" George asked.

Munch laughed. "No love there, I think. Magda was looking for the best security she could get. I tried, but Marvin Kell could give a little more. Now that Marvin is gone, I can give her better."

George looked at me and winked. "Where is Magda's family?"

Again he laughed. "I don't know. I met her in the yards. She worked there until Kell took her away."

"And you were upset when this happened?" I asked.

"Of course, I was. I approached Marvin Kell and we had several arguments, but Magda went with him."

"And they got married?"

"They did. It happened very quickly."

"She appears to have gotten pregnant very quickly."

"That is true as well, but I wonder who the father is?"

I shook my head. "What are you talking about, Mr. Munch?"

He smiled slyly. "When Marvin Kell was working at nights, sometimes his mother worked in the garment district, late shift. Magda would get lonely and come see me. You see, she loves me, not Marvin Kell."

This story was getting shakier by the moment. "Where were you the night Marvin was shot?"

"Very drunk at a tavern called The Pickle Barrel near the lumber yards. I have several friends who can tell you that I was there. I didn't hear about Marvin Kell until the next day."

I nodded. I believed Munch. "How do you communicate with her?"

He looked over at her and she smiled. He did something with his fingers and she responded by answering with her fingers and hands.

"She can't speak. I have a little brother with the same condition. I have to use sign language with both of them. It's the only way she can talk."

I thought about Christian Hanson, also a mute. "What about, Kell? How did he communicate?"

"She can hear and understand some things, like most of the mean things Mrs. Kell said about her. I think Marvin Kell was just nice to her and she understood most of it."

In the carriage ride back to the precinct, I looked over at George. "He is not a suspect. He's just a big, easy going guy who fell in love with a girl. When someone took her he may have gotten upset and said a few things, but that was it. When Kell died he took her back. I think our little Magda was just looking out for herself."

George smiled. "Who's the daddy?"

"Time and how the kid looks will tell. I wouldn't put any money on anyone just yet."

• • •

It had been a long day followed up by a marginal meal at Coopers. Not only was the food marginal, but no one visited me. I was able to eat in near silence. Only the conversation of other diners filled my ears. I didn't hear anything that interested me. When I was finished eating and had the last drop of my beer I headed home.

In the carriage I was able to focus on the weather. The temperature was still in the low eighties' the humidity was still high. There was no breeze from anywhere to counter any of this. It wasn't long that as the carriage rolled along I was drenched with sweat.

Stepping out of the cab in front of my building, I wasn't surprised to see a lone figure sitting on the stairs that led up to my apartment. As I got closer the woman looked up and smiled. She had a nice smile and I remembered soft lips.

"Good evening, Detective Moses," she said.

"Good evening, Miss McDermott."

I sat down next to her on the stairs and she leaned over and kissed me on the cheek. "I was hoping you wouldn't mind a little company."

"I never mind the company of a beautiful woman."

"Even if the woman is a prostitute?"

"If I make it up to Heaven and that's a big if, I don't think they'll be fitting me for angel's wings right away."

She giggled. "Eleanor said you weren't always such a good boy."

Eleanor Winter had been my first true love. No doubt that we'd be together today if a madman hadn't cut her up and left her to die. "I've had my battles," I said.

"Some say as a cop that you don't always follow the rules."

I thought of Captain Garfield and his crusade to find me guilty of murder. "I always try to do the right thing based on the circumstances at the time. It's not always easy."

"Eleanor also said that you were one of the nicest, sweetest people that she'd ever met."

I took Joan's hand. "I was taught a long time ago that it was always better to be nice to people. Also a lot easier than being mean and nasty to them."

"I ran away from home when I was thirteen. My father was always beating my mother. I would try and get him to stop and he would beat me. I snuck on a train from Nashville to Chicago and have been working ever since."

I thought of the stories of immigrants who got off trains and ended up drugged and forced into prostitution. My stomach roiled. "You're still young and smart. You don't have to stay in that life."

She laughed. "You're right, Detective. I was thinking of opening a bookkeeping office."

"You know what I mean."

She took my hand. "I do. Right now, I think that the only thing I was looking for was a little bit of friendship. Nothing more than that. Is that asking too much?"

It was dark but I was staring into her dark eyes. "I don't think so at all."

"Then why don't we head upstairs and have a little fun?"

She got up, still holding my hand. I didn't answer. I didn't need to. She led the way.

Day Five

I woke earlier than normal the following day. Joan McDermott was lying by my side, deep in sleep, a soft snore coming from her. She was a very pretty girl and I liked her. From what she has said, she came from a tormented home, one she had to get away from. It was like this with a lot of prostitutes. They had nowhere to go until the life found them. I wouldn't say saved them. Many died of drug and alcohol abuse, not to mention diseases. Nothing in that life seemed glamorous. Eleanor Winter found it hard to leave the life even though I had told her I would take care of her. Joan had laughed when I told her that she didn't have to stay living that way. I was clearly not understanding something.

My mother had been a prostitute. I had never known her. My father had gotten her pregnant. When I was born I was whisked away to Holy Trinity Orphanage. My mother was sent away as well. I later heard she may have gone to New York, but in my travels there I turned up nothing. All I have of her memory is an old, faded photograph. I also knew her name was Rose. Really a beautiful name.

During these thoughts I felt my eyes filling with tears. Several rolled down my face and onto my pillow. Why was it that I felt so damn alone? My three closest friends Father Luigi, Gunter Krause and Eleanor Winter had all left me in the last year. I felt for some time now that I hadn't done enough for all of them. I could have been there more for them. It left me with an overwhelming feeling of failure.

I got up quietly, cleaned up, left money for Joan for a carriage on the night table, and left my apartment. I was able to hail a cab on Clark Street and I instructed the driver to take me to Mercy Hospital. My last two trips there were to watch Luigi die and to talk with Beth Stokes after her husband, Amos, had beaten her. Today I wanted to see someone to help me understand.

It was just past six-thirty in the morning when I wandered up to the nurse's station on the first floor of the hospital. There were two nurses present. One appeared to be dozing. The other, a younger looking woman, looked up at me, clearly surprised.

"Oh, you startled me," she said.

"I'm sorry," I said. "I didn't mean to."

She was really young and I figured it had been because of this that she got the late night shift. "What can I do for you, sir?"

I didn't know Pinter's wife's name. "I'd like to see one of the patients. A Mrs. Pinter?"

She smiled. "I'm sorry, sir. We don't allow visitation until nine o'clock. You'll have to come back then."

I thought I'd play the charm game, but instead drew my badge. Her eyes opened a little wider. "I have to go on duty soon and I wanted to just see her. I understand that she is not doing well. I may not have another chance."

She looked up at my face and then the badge again. She checked a stack of papers. "Come with me, Detective," she said.

I followed her up two flights of stairs to the third floor. This floor was silent, not a sound. We walked about midway down the hall and she stopped, pointing to a room on her left. The name on the written sign said, 'Martha Pinter'. "Two minutes," she said.

I walked into the room and there lay Pinter's wife, Martha. A vision hit me and I was again looking at the large frame of Father Luigi on his death bed. Martha Pinter couldn't have been any paler. Her skin was a chalky white, her lips void of color. The thin hair on her head was all gray. One of her hands was outside on the bed sheet. It was all bone and veins. I wondered if any blood still coursed through them. I thought of Pinter. I thought of how hard he worked and I thought that work was his love. I had been stupid and arrogant, because all I had was work. Harold had another love and he was going to lose her soon. Tears hit me again and I sobbed. I wiped at my eyes with my sleeve.

I realized there in that terminal hospital ward that I missed love. I missed caring for someone. There was an aura around me that said that anyone who got close to me ended up dead. I had started to believe it and it had turned me inward. I started to think that I was incapable of love, but I knew that I was wrong.

I would always have my work. Did I love it? I hated evil and I meant to tame as much of it as possible. Taming evil. What a noble cause in a place like the Levee District. I had a lot to do and I would finish it all, but then I needed to try and find love. I needed that. Without it I had a sense that I might not survive. In the past I had turned to booze and opium to get me by. If that behavior continued I could see that I would die a young man.

•   •   •

Loftus and I had talked when I got into the precinct and it was decided that we would head over to the Everleigh Club around eleven in the morning. I knew that the two sisters, Minna and Ada, worked late, but were always up and dressed by eleven. They ran the most profitable house in the Levee; they worked it hard and it paid off.

"I think one of us should make a trip to St. Louis to find out what Patricia Farmer was up to at the school that she attended," Loftus said. He had made his way over to my desk and sat on the edge of it.

"You think that we'll find a similar story there?"

"I think I am losing sleep over it. We know what she did with Madeline Marsden and now we have a similar situation with Brian Albright. It's bothering me that we don't know what happened at the school down there."

"If anything happened."

"That's true, but when you transfer out of a school and move to Chicago it seems something might have happened."

"I can ask Shipley for approval for one of us to make the trip. It won't be costly, but the loss of time might affect the way he thinks."

George rubbed his chin; he hadn't shaved and the dark stubble was thickening. "He wants convictions. The only way to nail down the hardest sentence for Patricia is to find out more about her."

I agreed. "I'll talk with Shipley."

As George was headed back to his desk, a runner came upstairs to tell us that we had a visitor in the lobby. My first thought was that Mrs. Kell was making her daily update visit, but then the runner said it was Captain Bill Callahan from the 23rd Precinct. My thoughts switched quickly from Patricia Farmer to Marvin Kell. We both got up from our desks and headed downstairs.

•   •   •

Captain Bill Callahan said he wanted to speak with us privately. We led him to a first floor meeting room and the door was closed. I expected Callahan to sit, but he stood at the end of the long table in the room and placed both of his hands on the table, leaning forward. George and I both stood at the opposite end of the table.

"The stolen van from the other night was from our yard," he said. His face was flushed; he looked angry. "I can find nothing that says any officer from our precinct was involved in removing it from the yard."

"I'm not surprised," I said. "We have nothing that links the murder to anyone in your precinct other than the van."

"Not so fast, Detective," Callahan said. "You're getting ahead of yourself."

I let out a breath. "I didn't mean to."

Callahan relaxed his stance. Some of the tension seemed to leave his face. "There's an officer in our precinct who goes by the name of Gulliver. Joseph Gulliver. Used to be in the army. Used to be a boxer. He's a tough son of a bitch."

I knew Joey Gulliver and had boxed him several times. I really shouldn't say boxed because he knocked me down a number of times. He was mean and smiled at you while he boxed you. He took a lot of pleasure in beating the shit out of you.

"When I checked around the precinct I heard a number of stories about a conflict between Joe Gulliver and Marvin Kell. When I asked what the conflict was about I got the same answer every time. There was no reason for the conflict. These two men simply did not like each other."

"Have you talked personally to Gulliver about this?" I asked.

"No, I haven't. I didn't want to make him aware of anything and didn't want to cause any kind of ruckus in the precinct, but I heard enough about the problem to call it a legitimate reason to talk with Gulliver."

"What specifically did you hear?" George asked.

Callahan rolled his shoulders. The discussion had tightened him up. "At first I heard the two of them just traded barbs, insults. No one seems to know why, but most say Gulliver initiated these conflicts. These apparently went on for a while. Sometimes they were light hearted; other times they were mean spirited. Eventually, they got personal."

"How so?" I asked.

"For some reason, Joe Gulliver began to make fun of Kell's wife. I understand the insults became gutter based and quite vile. A source told me he was certain that Gulliver wanted to draw Kell into a fist fight."

This didn't sound like it was headed in the right direction. "Did he succeed?"

Bill Callahan smiled. "That's why I'm here. The fight occurred about ten days before Kell was gunned down."

"But if Joey punched out Kell in a fist fight, why would he then want to proceed to shooting him?"

Callahan gave me a sidelong glance. "You're misinformed, Detective Moses. It was a one punch fight. Kell threw it and landed it squarely on Gulliver's nose. It knocked him out and broke his nose. The fight lasted about ten seconds."

I whistled. Joey Gulliver was tough, but apparently not that tough. "Maybe we should have a talk with Joey," I said.

"That's why I am here," Callahan said.

•   •   •

I was still in a melancholy mood as we walked along Dearborn to the Everleigh Club. Nature had been a friend today and provided a thick cloud cover with rain possible. This cut down on the baking sun. As it was, it was still warm. The Levee was usually asleep from four in the morning until about noon. This was when the gamblers and drunks would appear in the neighborhood to lose their money in different ways. The ladies of the evening were always available, but were busier at night. I was told that this was due to people having to work during the day to pay for their services. This made sense.

"Do you have a family, George?" I asked.

"Everybody has a family somewhere," he said.

I had a mother and a father, one dead, one in an unknown spot; my wife and children gone in a fire.

"I didn't mean it that way," George said. "I mean, I know you grew up at Holy Trinity. I also know you were in my apartment once, trying to prove I was a killer. That should have also proven that I was a bachelor."

"It did," I said.

"My mother lives on the west side of the city; I see her once in a while. My father is dead. His heart gave out. I also have a sister that married some asshole in Ohio. He owns some sort of store. They have a couple of kids. I haven't seen her in several years."

"Never close?" I asked.

"She was quite a bit older, five, six years I think. We knew each other, but the age difference meant we were doing different things at different times. It was really hard to get to know one another."

"And your brother in law the asshole?"

"Some kind of bible banging type. Thinks God is going to take care of him and his family regardless of what happens. Should have been a preacher."

"What about you, George? Where does God come in your life?"

He stopped and stared at me. There was a little smile on his face. "I was raised a Catholic like you, Moses. I fear God and I pray to him, but not too much. If I ever need to pray to him when I'm in trouble I really want him to listen extra hard. That surprise you?"

"No," I said. "I try not to pray too much or ask God for anything. I think that he and I have a strained relationship, but I do hope he keeps an eye on me."

"Hasn't helped for some of the people that have been around you." George started off again down the street.

He was right, of course. The curse of being my partner lurked. I wasn't sure I could do a lot to make it any better. Maybe not getting one of them killed.

•　•　•

It was just past eleven when we got to the Everleigh Club. We were greeted by a black maid who told us that the sisters were having their breakfast in the dining room. When we showed our badges, she retreated to tell them that the police wanted to have a word with them.

The Everleigh Club is the one brothel that you can go in early in the morning and not have the smell of old booze and burnt cigars and cigarettes. Even this early in the day it smelled fresh and shined brightly. Everything seemed to have been cleaned or polished. The lighting in the place was brilliant.

"Been here, George?"

"Once when there was a disturbance. One of the ladies stabbed one of guests. He wasn't much of a gentleman from what I can remember. They say the Field kid got shot here by a whore."

"I wouldn't know anything about that," I said. George looked like he believed me so I said nothing further.

The maid came back to the foyer and motioned for us to follow. "Miss Ada and Miss Minna just finishin their breakfast. They said they'd talk to you in the dining room."

When we entered the dining room we found the two sisters seated at each end of a long table. The sisters, attractive in their own way, were dressed impeccably. They wore gowns that showed a fair amount of cleavage with enough jewelry to make you think of robbing them. They were both fully made up and ready for another long day as madams.

More than equal to the way they were dressed was the spread of food before them. The table was covered with bowls of fruit, plates of ham and bacon, a dish of scrambled eggs, toast, pancakes and I thought what looked like a tray of smoked fish. I hadn't eaten anything all day after arising so early. My mouth watered as I viewed the feast. George groaned and I thought I heard his stomach growl.

"Detective Moses," Ada Everleigh said, "you have a way of coming to our club on a regular basis without ever paying any money here." She smiled.

"I'm afraid I cannot afford many of the services that your fine club provides."

"I don't doubt that," Minna said. She was not smiling. "Another new partner?"

"This is Detective Loftus. New to me, but not new to the force."

"Coffee or tea, detectives?" Ada said. Minna gave her a scowl.

I would have sat down and devoured a good portion of the food on the table if I hadn't remembered why we were there. We weren't guests. "I appreciate that, but we are just here to ask a few questions and then we will be on our way."

Ada wiped her lips delicately with a cloth napkin. "Please ask away. We always aim to help the police."

"We're investigating the murder of Allen Price and his family," I said.

Ada popped a piece of melon into her mouth. "Certainly you don't think that Minna and I are suspects."

I laughed. "Why would we ever think something like that, Ada?"

"If the truth must be known, Allen Price was a vile person. He would come in here to play faro, which he wasn't very good at, and then complain to anyone who would listen that he was being cheated by the dealers or the house. On a night when he did win, he would want to go upstairs with one of the girls. This wouldn't have been a problem in most cases but he liked to get physical in a most unusual way."

I heard George stifle a laugh. "Would you care to embellish?" I asked.

"He was a biter, Detective," Minna said.

"Excuse me?" I said.

"Minna is right, Detective Moses. Allen Price bit three of our girls, two on the shoulder, and one on the back of the neck."

"What the fuck?" George said.

"Please, your language, Detective," Ada said.

"I'm sorry," George said. "He blushed.

"Let's get back to the biting. Are you saying that Allen Price actually bit these girls?" I asked.

"Broke the skin on two occasions and drew some blood," Ada said. "Like a vampire."

"Wouldn't once have been enough?" I said.

"In most cases. Allen Price lost a lot of money at our tables. He was a good customer despite his complaining. In every case where he bit someone he also gave them a handsome bonus."

"So you were condoning his actions?"

"Not really," Ada said. "The situation policed itself. We had no more girls who would go upstairs with Allen. Apparently getting a tip or a bonus does not compensate for getting bitten.

I shook my head. "Okay, forget the biting. Let's get back to the faro games. We heard that Price had an incident with some dealers who he accused of cheating him."

"That was towards the end of the year," Minna said. "He accused the Allard brothers of cheating him. He made a big fuss about it, caused a big public scene. We had to ask him to leave and not to come back. Between the biting of the girls and his insistent complaining we had enough of Allen Price. He was more trouble than he was worth."

"So you kicked Allen out. What about the Allard brothers?"

Minna made some sort of grunting noise and waved a hand at me. "Ada can answer that one."

"I tried to give them a chance," Ada said. "They were nice boys, John and Jake. Very nice looking and very polite, but they had a past and I let them have a chance."

"What kind of past?" George asked.

"This is all my fault, but both had had problems dealing in the District before. There were reports of the two of them arguing with customers and even a fight in one casino. There was also some talk of cheating going on. They came to see me and I listened to them. I believed them and I took them on. There really wasn't much to go on before Allen Price started complaining. All of a sudden, he accuses both brothers. Minna and I had a deal that if a complaint came in about them I would have to let them go. So I did."

"Tell the nice officers the rest," Minna said.

Ada gave her sister a dirty look. "We found out later that both brothers had a criminal past as well. Both had done time in Indiana for armed robbery."

George and I looked at each other. George whistled. "I don't suppose that you might know where we can find these two brothers?"

"John had an apartment over on 20th Street. I heard Jake was staying with a girlfriend. I can get you the last address for John."

"That would be great, Ada," I said.

"Don't get us wrong, Detective Moses," Minna said. "We feel awful about what happened to Allen Price and his family. That's a terrible thing, but the way that Allen acted and did some things it wouldn't surprise us if he had many enemies and people who would want to get even with him."

"You mean like these Allard brothers?"

"Detective Moses, I told Ada not to hire those two boys. I knew they were bad news, but if Allen Price doesn't start shooting his mouth off about them cheating him then there is a good chance that both of them are still working here."

•   •   •

With the address the sisters gave us we headed for John Allard's apartment on 20th Street. Ada Everleigh told us that he went by Johnny. When we got to the apartment building we noticed that it was several units on top of a small gambling parlor. The building was only two stories tall with four units on the second floor. We climbed the stairs and I immediately noticed the old, musty smell in the stair case.

On the landing at the top of the stairs lay a dead mouse. Flies were mounting on the dead rodent.

The hall ran down between the four units; there were two on each side. There was no identification as to who lived in the units. We knocked on the first door on the left. We did so a number of times with no answer. We tried the door on the right. After pounding loudly the door was opened by a woman in a worn out robe opened loosely in the front. She had gnarly blonde, twisted hair. Her makeup was drying and caked on her face.

"What do you want?" she said.

I pushed my badge in her face, doubting it was the first time she'd seen one. "We're looking for Johnny Allard."

"Do I look like his fucking mother?" she said. Her eyes flared.

George reached across and grabbed her by the face. "I hope not," he said, "but I don't give a shit about what you look like. We need Johnny Allard."

Now the look on her face was something like terror. She raised her hand and pointed down the hall. George released his grip. She rubbed her jaw. "Down there. On the left."

"Learn some manners," George said. She closed her door.

"Learn that in the Catholic schools?" I said.

"Stupid whore," George mumbled.

At the end of the hall there was a collection of garbage that had collected under a window that led out to a set of stairs behind the building. I didn't see any more dead rodents, but this building clearly wasn't on the high end list.

George pounded on Johnny Allard's apartment door. He tried again, pounding hard and many times.

"Maybe he's not home," I said.

George pounded again and we were about to leave when the door was opened several inches. We could see one eye peering out at us. "I'm sleeping," a nervous voice said.

"Johnny Allard?" I said.

"I gotta sleep. I gotta work today at four," the voice said.

This time it was me who applied the force to the door and pushed it open. Johnny Allard backed up and almost fell on his back side. He didn't looked fully awake and then I realized he wasn't sober. His eyes were glazed over and he was sweating profusely. His short dark hair was beaded with sweat drops.

"Using something, Johnny?" I asked.

He wrapped his arms around him. "No. Just trying to get some sleep. I didn't do anything wrong."

"Nobody said you did anything," George added. "We just want to ask some questions."

The look he gave us showed he didn't believe us, but then he might have been just disoriented. "Word has it the got you into a beef with Allen Price over at the Everleigh Club," I said.

"Price? That son of a bitch cost me and Jake our jobs over there. He said we were cheating. We didn't cheat him. He was just a terrible player." His voice came out like a shriek, piercing.

"Tell us what happened."

Johnny shivered now and I wondered how sick he was or how drugged up. "Price lost big one night and gets up saying how me and Jake cheated him. Said we cheated him every time that he sat at our tables. He was real loud about it and the sisters kicked him out and then they fired Jake and me. Said they couldn't tolerate any of that kind of talk in their club."

"Did you and your brother ever cheat Allen Price?" George asked.

"Me, never. I don't know about Jake. He said he didn't, but I don't know for sure. Me and Jake don't always get along." He was still shivering.

"What are you using?" I asked.

He shook his head. "Just a little laudanum. It helps me sleep. I'm just a little short tonight."

I nodded. "When was the last time you saw Jake?'

"I don't know. Maybe four, five months ago. Like I said, we aren't that close. We don't always agree."

"We heard you went down for an armed robbery charge?"

"No. Not me. That was all Jake, back in Indiana. I've never had a record. I got us the jobs at Everleigh. Jake and me were okay until we got fired and he blamed me for the Price thing."

"Did you know someone blew Allen Price's head off?" I asked.

His look told the truth. He didn't know. "That's why you're here?"

"We heard about the fight at the Everleigh Club. We had to ask."

Johnny laughed. "Not me, Detectives."

"What about Jake?"

"Don't know anything about something like that."

"Know where we can find him?"

"He did live with a girl named Maggie. They were living above The Parlor on State. He was dealing there, I think. You gotta watch him, though. He's always got a gun and for some time I didn't think he was right."

I took a five dollar bill out of my pocket and gave it to him. "Try to get some sleep and try and get something to eat. You look like hell. You've got to take a break from the laudanum."

He nodded and wiped at his seeping nose. "Okay," he said.

Back out on the street, it was hard to get the smell of the building out of my nose. Where the Everleigh Club always smelled fresh, most places in the Levee smelled like yesterday's trash.

"You know he's just going to use that money that you gave him to buy more stuff?" George said.

"Maybe," I said. "He seemed like a good fellow."

"You've got a soft heart for addicts?"

"I've been there, George. I know the dependent feeling. Some are lucky to walk away and get straight. I've walked away, but can't say I won't go back. Sometimes you feel like you can't go on. The drugs make it feel better."

"Until you get trapped," George said.

I looked at him. He wasn't joking. "Maybe we should go and see if Jake Allard is home. He sounds like a better suspect than Johnny."

George patted me on the shoulder. "Let's go take a look."

• • •

The Parlor was another low level casino on State Street. Compared to the Everleigh Club there weren't many that weren't low level. I'd been in The Parlor one time when I was a patrolman. A woman had been sexually attacked by a gentleman in the back of the place. She took exception to the attack and used a fire place poker to bash him in the head. When we got to the casino the man was face down on a blackjack table with his skull caved in. The lady was sitting calmly at the next table, smoking a cigarette.

Today we weren't interested in the casino, but the apartments that were upstairs on the second floor. We found a janitor cleaning up the casino and he told us what unit Jake Allard lived in. Heeding what Johnny had told us, we approached the unit with our guns drawn. The quote about Jake not being right was a bit of an alarm. That and the fact that he always had a gun.

For some reason, we stood to the side of Jake's door as we pounded on it. There was no sound from within. We pounded again and a voice came from the inside. "What do you want?" A male voice, gruff.

George may have made a tactical error when he answered. "Police. We have some questions for Jake Allard."

We waited maybe twenty seconds with no answer and George pounded on the door again. This time the answer was a large caliber pistol being fired through the door, one shot. We both instinctively ducked and hit the floor. George's hat came off and lay between us. The one side of it had been hit and shredded by the bullet. An inch the other way takes George's head off.

"Look at my God damn hat," George said.

"Could have been your head," I said. I pounded on the door while lying on the floor.

Whoever was on the other side decided enough was enough and fired his remaining five shots through the upper half of the door and over our heads. I made sure to count carefully and stood and kicked the door in. I charged in ready to shoot.

Jake Allard was sitting at a table drinking whiskey from a small bottle. He was dressed only in his underwear. His unshaven face and blood shot eyes stared back at me as I came forward. He pointed the gun again and pulled the trigger, but got what I hoped for. It was empty.

I swung my own gun and hit him on top of the head. He fell hard to his left and landed on the floor. His gun slid away from him as he hit the floor. He was clearly drunk, but I had not knocked him out. I saw him squirming a bit and talking a stream of garbage.

George was standing behind me and was keeping an eye on Jake when a woman appeared from another room and swung a big, iron frying pan at George. Luckily, it hit him on the shoulder and he was able to turn and punch the woman squarely on the jaw. She stood for a moment and then fell backward, out cold.

"I guess that's Maggie," I said.

"Son of a bitch, Moses. First my hat and then some crazy bitch tries to kill me with a frying pan."

I smiled. "But you are alive and I didn't get you killed."

"Son of a bitch," George said. "You've gotten me locked up, involved in a stand- off and now shot at."

"I'm sorry, George. Maybe we should get these two cuffed and into the precinct so that we can figure out what they know about Allen Price."

"They must have been up to something. You just don't start shooting and swinging frying pans if you're law abiding citizens."

I looked down at Maggie, still out cold, and Jake Allard, moving but mumbling. Neither looked like a law abiding anything at the moment. I was just grateful that we didn't have a hole in us.

• • •

By the time we were finished processing the arrests of Jake Allard and Maggie it was almost mid-afternoon. Once Jake was in his cell he laid on the bunk and quickly fell asleep. Maggie was a little different. She was equally as drunk as Jake, but not quite ready for a nap. She yelled at us the entire time she was being processed and when we put her in her cell. She said loudly several times that she was friends with Alderman John Coughlin, one of the bosses of the Levee. She also moaned about a pain in her jaw. I was thinking that George had broken it when he punched her.

"We can question them both later after they sober up and can understand what the hell we went and saw them for," I said.

"Even if they had nothing to do with Price's murder they are going to sit for a bit for trying to kill two police detectives," George said.

"Attempted murder is not a charge that is that farfetched."

"I've got to eat," George said. "Knocking out a woman has a way of building an appetite."

"I'm only giving you some leeway on your actions because the gal was armed with a frying pan."

"Still doesn't mean I'm not hungry."

We stopped at a little place on Dearborn and both decided to get eggs with potatoes and toast. It was a lot better than most of the meals that I had eaten recently and the coffee helped me wake up a bit after my adrenaline high from the shooting had worn off.

"What do you think?" I asked George.

"It's either Joey Gulliver on the Kell murder or we can go back to see Thomas Vance about any other potential clients that Price either lost money on or used their investment money to gamble with."

I finished my coffee. Both Vance and Joey Gulliver would probably still be working. Gulliver could be anywhere on the streets. If Thomas Vance was working in all probability he was in his office on LaSalle Street. "Let's call Vance's office to make sure he's in before we head to the Loop. We can catch up with Joey later or in the morning."

"You think there's much of a chance that the murderers came from some connection to a jilted client of Price? It occurred to me, that after meeting Jake Allard, the killers would be somebody more like him."

That had occurred to me. Were people who had enough money to invest in commodities the likely kind to murder a whole family? It did seem the type would be more like Allard, somebody who would shoot at cops through a closed door. "Let's go see Vance. We have nothing yet. It would be wrong to leave anything unturned."

•　　•　　•

We found Thomas Vance back in his office on LaSalle Street. He looked like he had also returned from a late lunch. There was a large stain on his vest. Vance didn't look overly happy to see us and his first comment confirmed that.

"I told you officers everything that I knew about Allen Price," he said. We were seated in his office in front of his enormous desk. "I have a busy afternoon."

"This won't take long. We heard something that peeked our interest, something that maybe you forgot to tell us," I said.

"I wouldn't deliberately hold anything back from the police," he said. He stood up straight and tall in his chair.

"I didn't say it was deliberate. I said you may have forgotten to tell us."

"What would that be?" His face was turning beet red.

"We heard from a source that it was possible that Allen Price had used some investor money to gamble with."

Now Vance looked stunned. "That is the most preposterous thing that I have ever heard."

"You're denying it?" I said.

"Absolutely."

"George," I said.

"Mr. Vance," George said, "we are going to need the list of clients or investors that placed money with Allen Price for the past three years. Since you don't seem to know anything about what we are asking we will have to contact the investors on our own."

"What?" Vance boomed. "That is almost an impossible task."

"You don't keep records?" I asked.

"Of course we keep records."

"Then we need to see them," I said.

Vance crossed his thick arms over his large belly. "Who made this claim?"

"Mr. Vance," I said, "that doesn't matter. The fact is we heard it and we are here to investigate it. If Allen Price was using investor money to gamble and one of the investors heard about it that might give them a good reason to want to kill him. Do you see our point?"

Little droplets of sweat appeared on Vance's forehead. He closed his eyes for a moment and then reopened them. "We had a situation with Allen last year."

"What kind of situation?" George said.

"We found out twice that Allen had used investor money to gamble with. Allen took in some cash investments from two clients and used that money to finance his gambling. We found out about it and addressed the situation with Allen. Allen replaced all of the money in the investor's accounts."

"And how did the investor's react when they learned this?" I asked.

"They didn't. They never heard about it. We became aware of the violation and handled it privately with Allen."

""And the investors never found out?"

"No, never. We could have gotten in serious trouble had they found out and our reputation could have gone right down the sewer."

"But you didn't penalize Allen Price?"

"Again, Allen was a valued producer of ours. We gave him a stern warning that if this behavior ever happened again he would be let go. Thankfully, nothing like this ever happened again."

"And there was no harm to the investors?"

"Maybe a delay in getting their cash into the market, but it was not very much. The rest of the matter was handled discreetly. Like I said, if word of this transgression got out we could have been in serious trouble."

Looking for a carriage on LaSalle, I turned to George. "Guess we better hope that Jake Allard gives us a little more than the jilted investor theory."

"It was thin to begin with, but we learned one more thing. Allen Price would do just about anything to get ahead."

• • • •

There's lonely and then there is being alone. They are different. One can make you feel very sad. The other is something everyone seeks once in a while. That night I wanted to be alone. I felt my head was clear and I wanted to keep it that way. Looking at the two Allard brothers, one an addict, the other a drunk, made me think of the demons that I had fought. These days I was trying to temper the amount of alcohol that I put in my body and so far I was being good.

The fact that I could still imagine the opium pipe in my mouth and the taste of it made me scared. I wasn't that far from being an addict myself.

It was a quiet night at Coopers. Most of the time the place drew a good sized crowd and there were always loud mouths at the bar, but not tonight. Tonight my old standby seemed to be cooperating with me. Technically Loftus and I had three cases to work on and try and resolve. None of those seemed to be moving very quickly, but I thought there was some promise.

The most nagging and ridiculous was the case of Madeline Marsden and Patricia Farmer, the two teen-aged murderesses. Both were clearly present as the girls took the lives of three elderly women, but now one claimed she did nothing during the murders except draw pictures. This is what maybe anyone accused of a crime might say, but in this case there was a remarkable happening. In this case the other defendant agreed. Madeline Marsden said that she did all the dirty work while Patricia Farmer sat by and doodled. I shook my head.

I had seen Lieutenant Shipley before I left the precinct and told him about securing more information on Patricia Farmer by going to St. Louis. He wasn't excited about losing the manpower for two days, but we decided George would be alright and I told Shipley I would clear up any live leads before I left. I thought that could be accomplished in the morning. There was an evening train tomorrow and I would be on it.

The other two cases, simple murders, if you will, were not at a standstill. I actually felt we were generating a little momentum and getting somewhere. The Price murders clearly looked like a robbery gone bad. It was unclear if anything had actually been taken from the house. What was clear was that more than one person had committed the crime. When you look at suspects, you have to look at motive. Jake Allard had motive. Price had led to his firing at the Everleigh Club. Allard knew Price had money and maybe went looking for it. Finding nothing in the house, Allard and associates killed the family in rage. I felt Jake Allard had the temperament to kill. He had no problem firing his gun at George and me as we knocked on his apartment door. Even crazy Maggie with her frying pan might figure into it. She didn't seem to be quite normal either. They were on the list for George and me to talk with in the morning.

Our other conversation tomorrow would be with Joey Gulliver. Joey was a tough guy and a talented boxer, but apparently not as tough as Marvin Kell had been. I had a real hard time believing that Joey could be a cold blooded murderer, but Marvin had given him motive by knocking him out in a public fist fight. Maybe Joey recovered mentally and decided the only payback for Marvin was to take him out permanently. I had seen sicker things happen, but this one I doubted.

Other than a yet to be found bullet slug and some fake hair strands from a black wig we didn't have much more to go on with Marvin Kell's murder. The stolen police van had yielded nothing further than the hairs. Frederick Munch, who regained the pregnant Magda, seemed like a prospect, but he wasn't a killer. Maybe the talk with Joey would tell us something, but I wasn't very encouraged.

Not really much of an issue, but the thoughts of Captain Garfield and Christian Hanson were never too far away. One wanted to ruin my career; the other wanted to kill me. I didn't think Garfield would ever find anything to have enough on me to cause any trouble, but he wasn't going to go away. With Hanson, if he was around, I knew he would try something again. It was just a matter of when.

In the carriage on the way home we drove past Soon Lee's, the Chinese food place with the opium den in the basement. Again I felt I could smell and taste the drug and feel the effects, but that was nonsense. I turned and looked the other way out of the carriage.

When I got out of the carriage I looked up in the sky and watched as a lone cloud drifted past a full moon. Full moons meant crazy things happened. I laughed. Crazy things always happened in the Levee and it didn't matter what kind of moon we had. I also looked to the porch in front of my building. I had wanted to be alone, but I had a feeling Joan McDermott might be waiting for me, but she wasn't. I had succeeded in being alone for the evening, but now the feeling was sliding towards loneliness. The only cure for this was bed and going to sleep.

Day Six

We got to the 23rd Precinct before their nine o'clock roll call where assignments would be handed out to the patrolmen for the day. Like us, Joey Gulliver was a detective with over ten years on the force. Other than being noted as a tough guy he had no blemishes on his record. He had been rewarded a couple of times for bravery in the line of duty. To call him a model cop might be exaggerating because I knew Joey. He wasn't an orphan like me, but he grew up tough. I hadn't seen him in close to eight years, the last time we fought. I was surprised.

Joey was several inches shorter than me, but built with thick arms, legs and neck. He looked like a two legged bull. Today, he still had a lot of the thickness, but there was a pretty substantial roll of fat above his straining belt. There were also signs of the recently broken nose as some of the bruising remained around his eyes. He wasn't smiling when he met us in an office on the second floor of the precinct.

"Moses, I hear you are quite the cop these days, solving crimes, kicking ass and shooting people good or bad," he said.

I closed the office door behind me. I wasn't sure where the tone of this meeting might take us. "How have you been, Joey?"

"Other than talking to you, I've been fine, but the Captain said I had to see you so here I am."

I pointed at his facial bruising. "Still boxing, Joey?"

"Whenever some punk thinks he can take me."

"Was that what it was with Marvin Kell? Did Marvin think he could take you?"

Joey waved a hand at me and said to George. "Your partner and I have a history in the ring. I kicked his ass a few times."

"Be careful. He'll shoot you," George said.

"What about your beef with Marvin Kell?" I asked.

Joey shrugged. "Wasn't really much of a beef. We didn't like each other from the first day the kid walked in here. I gave him jabs and he gave them back."

"Why didn't you like him?"

"Don't know. Maybe I thought he was a smart ass rookie. A know it all. Cocky. You know the type, Moses. I heard you were like that."

"And you never liked me?"

A smile. "Not much."

"Okay. We have established the point that the two of us weren't best friends. What about the fight?"

Joey pointed to his nose. "Not much of a fight that I remember. I made some sort of crack to him, don't remember what, and he cold cocked me."

Now I smiled. "You let somebody sucker punch you, Joey?"

Another shrug. "It happens. Say, what is this all about, Moses?"

"Well, Detective Loftus and I are trying to figure out who walked up to Marvin Kell and shot him in the head and then drove off in a police van."

"So why the fuck are you talking with me?"

"We were told that you had a prickly relationship with the deceased."

"Are you guys fucking kidding me? Do you actually think that I would be the one to murder Marvin Kell?"

"Joey, we are looking at anyone who might have had an issue with Marvin Kell. You seem to fit that criteria."

Joey laughed. "Fine. I thought Marvin Kell was a jerk. I didn't like him. We traded insults regularly and the guy took offense and punched me out. Those are the facts, but I had nothing to do with the bastard's murder. It actually made me sick."

"The standard question, Joey. Where were you when Kell was killed?"

"You know, Moses, I used to drink and once in a while I used to try and bed a few women, but my lovely wife didn't care for this. She said if I ever came home smelling like perfume again that she would stick me in the gut with a carving knife. There was something in her tone that made me believe her. I stopped the booze and the women that night. If you want you can ask her, but at two o'clock in the morning on the day Kell was murdered, I was sleeping next to Julia."

I liked Joey about as much as he liked me, but I believed him. "Anybody else around here who might have wanted to kill Marvin?"

"I actually kept hearing what a nice guy he was. I was the only one who seemed to be at odds with him."

Any leads we had went down to zero, I thought.

"You know, Loftus," Joey said, "Moses here was a pretty good boxer. I beat him up, but he beat everybody else. He could have made money at it."

George smiled. "I heard some of that."

"Now he works in the fucking Levee District, trying to figure out who is the most scummy from all of the scum."

"I'm right there with him," George said.

"Yeah, I hear you. And all that shit about Moses shooting innocent people, that's bullshit. I've heard and known about him for over ten years. The right people will tell you that he's a good cop. The others' won't. If he shot someone, they deserved it."

Walking out of the precinct, George turned to me. "Joey Gulliver makes you sound like a choir boy."

"Don't believe him."

"Just don't get me killed, Moses. It was close with Jake Allard."

"Let's go see why he was shooting at us and why Maggie tried to smash your head in with that frying pan."

* * *

"You can't hold me in here forever," Maggie said. "I didn't do anything and you just can't hold me in here." At one time she might have been an attractive woman, but age and booze had caught up with her. There were deep lines on her face and dark circles surrounded her eyes. Her hair was blonde colored, but at the roots there was black and gray showing through. She had an enormous bosom, but also sported a good sized stomach. Even though she appeared completely sober the cell smelled of cigarettes and old gin.

"It might be smart of you to let me walk out of here," she continued. "I wouldn't want to have to report the both of you to Alderman John Coughlin, my good friend.

George lit a cigarette and gave it to her. She took it and started puffing without offering any thanks for it. She flicked an ash on the floor.

"You don't know why we are holding you?" I said. "You don't recall why you were arrested?"

She stared at me and pointed the cigarette at me. "I have done nothing wrong. You just can't hold me."

"We have arrested you for an assault on a police officer," I said. "Yesterday afternoon you attempted to behead Detective Loftus with a rather large and heavy frying pan."

She looked at Loftus. "He looks perfectly fine to me."

"Because you missed most of him."

"I don't believe you," she said.

"Doesn't matter. Detective Loftus and I both witnessed the attack."

"Alderman Coughlin will believe me."

"I doubt it. The man admittedly doesn't like me, but he's not going to take your word over two police officers," I said.

"You could be looking at maybe five years in the women's section of the county prison," George said. "You been there, Maggie?"

She looked again at Loftus and then back to me. "You're not going to get at me with your fucking threats," she said.

"No threats, Maggie," I said. "You think we're fucking idiots? You were so drunk you don't remember anything. You swung the frying pan after Loftus and I came in the apartment when your boyfriend ran out of bullets. I don't give a shit if you want to play tough and tell us who you know. That's all bullshit. Makes no difference to me if you go to county. The dykes will like someone as pretty as you."

She raised the smoke to her mouth and took a drag. I noticed that her hand was shaking.

"Like I said, I don't care what happens to you, but do you think we're spending all of this time in this rotten cell because you swung a frying pan at Loftus? Do you think that's why we are really here?" I asked.

Another drag on the smoke. "Okay," she said. "What do you two assholes want?"

"Now we are assholes," George said. "I gave you a fucking cigarette."

She smiled and blew smoke at him.

"What's your relationship with Jake Allard?" I asked.

She shrugged. "We spend time together. We have fun."

"Been together a while, we've heard."

"It's been a while. That's my place you came to. I got Jake a job dealing faro downstairs. I manage the place now and then."

"Nice place," I said.

"Okay, Detective Moses. What do you want?"

"Ever hear the name Allen Price?"

"Sure. Big shot businessman who got shot up."

"Not shot up," I said. "Shot gunned. Somebody killed that whole family. We are trying to figure out who did it."

She finished the smoke and flipped the bud on the floor. "So why are you talking to me?"

"It's not you I give a shit about," I said. "I want you to tell us what you know about Jake's whereabouts the night of the murders."

She looked horrified. "Jake wouldn't do anything like that. He's not that crazy."

"He was crazy enough to empty his revolver at us," George said. He offered Maggie another smoke, but she waved him off.

"But he wouldn't have anything to do with killing a whole family. That's not Jake."

"So where was he that night?" I asked. "We can help you out if you help us."

"I don't know where he was. He told me he had a bunch of errands to run and when I came in from the casino he was sleeping. That was about two in the morning. He'd had some drinks. I tried to rouse him." She smiled again.

I bent down so I was looking her right in the eye. "Really, Maggie, no idea where he was? I want you to think about this answer. The frying pan thing we can look past, but if we find that you lied to us about what you know about Allen Price, that is going to make me mad. I will make sure they bury that key to the women's ward. You might not get out."

"Jake told me he had to run some errands. I believed him. I came upstairs and he was asleep. The next day he seemed fine. He had to work. We didn't discuss anything further. That is what I know. That is the truth."

I didn't like her in the least, but I thought she was telling the truth. Jake could have done the dirty deed at Allen Price's house and come back to the apartment and fallen asleep. Cold blooded killers could do stuff like that. We wouldn't know much more until we talked with Jake. "Cut her loose," I said.

"You're not going to charge her for trying to take my head off?" George said.

I smiled. "Too much paperwork."

Now it was George's turn to bend down close to her face. "Swing a fucking frying pan at me again and you have my word that I will shoot you in the fucking head."

There was a look on Maggie's face. I wouldn't call it fear. She smiled. "Next time I might not miss, Detective Loftus."

• • •

Before we met with Jake Allard, I stopped in Harold Pinter's lab to see what he was up to. As usual, he was busy peeking through his microscope at something and didn't hear me enter the room.

"I'm not interrupting, am I?" I asked.

Harold looked up from his viewing and pushed his glasses back on his nose. "Not really, Patrick. They have new and better equipment out there these days, but so far our department doesn't see the need for funding the criminology lab."

"Science doesn't matter, I take it."

"Unfortunately, many views that are out there are still deemed to be closer to witchcraft. Old timers view crime solving as hitting the streets and finding suspects."

"I see it that way, too, but I will listen to anything that pushes me in the right direction."

Harold smiled. "You're a smart boy," he said. "I don't have much to tell you on either Price or Kell. I was able to get the coroner to give me the bullet that killed Kell. The shell and most of the jacket fragmented badly when it hit the skull, but I am convinced that it was fired from a .38 caliber at a close range."

I nodded. "And the dark hairs?"

"Find someone in this city who owns a black wig and maybe they are a suspect."

"Science isn't telling me much today."

"Like I said, I don't have much to offer."

"I stopped by Mercy and checked on your wife," I said. As soon as I did I wondered if I was breaching too personal an issue.

Harold lowered his gaze to the microscope. "That was nice of you."

"I will say that she looked very peaceful."

He looked back at me. "The wonder of pain killing drugs. At this point that is all that we can do for her. I want her to be as comfortable as possible."

"I never asked and it's probably none of my business, but do you have any children?"

Harold's eyes seemed to glaze over for a moment. "We have a son. He lives in Denver. I haven't seen him in over ten years. I got into a terrible argument with him and he moved away. I have sent him telegrams about his mother's condition, but he has yet to respond. I don't want him to regret that he didn't see her before she goes."

"I assume that you are mostly to blame for the argument?"

"Steven told us something one night of a personal nature regarding his relationships. I was at first disgusted with what he said and then I became angry. That little disagreement cost me my relationship with my son. My poor wife has always stood in the middle, not taking sides. I fear she will go with the issue never resolved."

"Is there anything I can do for you and your wife?" My comment seemed a little hollow.

"Just pray, Patrick. Prayer is the only thing that can help at a time like this."

I nodded. My relationship with God had taken a tumble over the past year, but the least I could do was offer up something for Harold's dying wife and estranged son. "I can do that," I said. He put his eyes back into the scope's viewer and I left the room.

•   •   •

Jake Allard was being held in a familiar cell. Right after Christmas a sick man named George Pelicanos had hanged himself in there after admitting to some crimes that he hadn't committed. Before I had left for New York in January, I had sent his wife some money. When I came back to Chicago I had checked on her, but she was gone. Now the cell was occupied by Jake. He wasn't dead, but he didn't look very alive. He was sitting on the cell's bunk staring vacantly ahead of him. When we opened the cell and got closer to him we could see him clearly and smell him.

Jake Allard looked like a sick man. Not drug sick like his brother, but alcoholic sick. His skin had a yellow pallor and I wondered if his liver was giving out. His hair, black and gray, was streaked with sweat. His white undershirt was dirty and stains showed under the arm pits. The smell coming from Jake was somewhere between old onions and bad booze mixed with perspiration. I wondered how this talk was going to go.

"You know why you are here, Jake?" I asked.

He peered up at me with bloodshot eyes. "Probably that damn Maggie. Probably saying that I hit her again."

"He doesn't even remember yesterday," George said.

"You don't remember shooting at us when we came to see you at Maggie's apartment?" I asked.

Now he gave me a vacant, lost look. "Why the hell would I shoot at two police officers? That might be more stupid than anything."

"Forget yesterday. Do you recall when you had a job at the Everleigh Club?"

He smiled. "Yeah, I remember that. Wasn't too long ago."

"Remember why you were fired?"

He scrunched his eyes shut for a moment. "Me and Johnny got in trouble because some rich bastard said we had cheated him at the faro table. Bastard said we cheated but this was the worst faro player I ever saw."

"Remember the rich bastard's name?"

Again the eye scrunching. "Sure. Allen fucking Price. That was a good job, too. Johnny and me we were doing okay there. We were watching what we did, you know, not much dope and watching the booze for me. We were getting better. Then we got fired and it's been a little rough."

Both John and Jake Allard looked like they'd fallen into an abyss since the firing. "Maggie said you were working for her?"

"A little dealing, but mostly I only sweep up and clean the joint."

"You do know what happened to Allen Price?"

He looked at me, a frightened look on his face. "I can't talk about that with anybody."

"What the fuck," George said loudly.

I silenced him with my hand. "What do you mean you can't talk about what happened to Allen Price with anybody?"

He smiled a little. "Well, I don't want to be getting myself into any trouble."

With that, George took a big step forward and grabbed Jake by his undershirt and pulled him off the bunk. He pulled him upward, but George was still looking down at him; Jake looked shocked. "Listen to me, you drunken sod. You had better tell us what you know about what happened to Allen Price right now or things are going to get very bad for you."

"Easy, George," I said. "Let him go."

George relaxed and pushed Jake back onto the bunk. "You owe me a new fucking hat."

Now Jake looked scared and confused. "What?"

"Forget that," I said. "Tell us about Allen Price."

Jake took a breath. "He was playing faro at the Everleigh Club a while back. I wasn't dealing. I was at the bar. Price was having a good night. He was winning big. When he started winning, which wasn't much, he would talk about taking his winnings and putting them into his big safe at home. He said when he had enough he was going to come back and try and break the bank."

"Wait a minute, Jake," I said. "We were told Allen was always losing. We heard that he always had to borrow to cover his debts. I'm not sure he had this big safe at home where he stored money."

Jake shook his head. "He never did. He might have won one night out of ten. I knew there was no safe at home where he had money stored up. He was always losing and having to borrow to play."

Now it was my turn to shake my head. "What are you talking about, Jake? What couldn't you tell us about Allen Price that might get you into trouble?"

"You wouldn't let me tell my damn story," he said.

"Just tell us what you know before I strangle you," George said. His face was a nice shade of red.

"Okay, you gotta listen though."

George backed up and crossed his arms over his chest. "Go ahead," I said.

Jake wiped his nose and mouth with the sleeve of his shirt. "Like I said I wasn't dealing. I was by the bar and Price was talking loudly about stuffing this money into his safe, saving so he could come back and break the bank."

"We got that part," George said.

"There were these two guys standing by the bar listening to Price shooting his mouth off. They were both having drinks, right by where I was standing."

"Who were these guys?" I asked.

"I have no idea," Jake said. "Both of them were dressed pretty good. They looked like they had a little money."

"Ever see them before in the club?"

"Not that I can remember. Sometimes I remember people at the tables if I'm dealing, but guys who just come in to have a drink I don't. There's too many of them."

"What was it about the two men that you do remember?"

Jake reached up and pushed back the sweat soaked front of his hair. He didn't look healthy. "I heard the one guy say to the other something like, 'do you hear that guy bragging about this safe he has in his house with a lot of money in it?' "

"What did the other guys say?"

"He seemed more relaxed about what Price was saying. He was smoking a cigar and sipping bourbon. He said something like, 'I hear him'."

"That was it?" George said.

"Give me a little time to think about it," Jake said. His face seemed flushed. "The first guy asked if he thought the guy bragging was telling the truth. The second guy said the only way they would ever figure this out was to pay the guy a visit and see for themselves."

"He said that for sure?" I asked.

"That's what I remember."

"But you don't remember anything about how they looked?" George said.

"I didn't say that. The guy with the cigar was missing half of his ear. It was on the side nearest to me so it must have been his right ear."

"Nothing more?" I said.

"That's all."

"Why were you afraid to tell us this?"

"The guy smoking the cigar and missing half of his ear looked real serious. He wasn't smiling or nothing. When a couple of the girls came by he was very rude to them. With the ear missing and his surly attitude, he seemed like the kind of guy to get even if you crossed him. I don't want those two to know that I told you anything."

Jake Allard looked frightened. "We won't say anything to them if we ever meet them," I said.

"Did they ever rob this Price fellow, looking for his safe?" Jake asked.

"We don't know if it was these two guys who were involved but somebody did pay a visit to Allen Price. Whoever it was blew a good part of Price's head off and then killed his wife and kids."

"Oh, my," Allard said."

We were back at our desk, writing down the notes of our visits to Maggie and Jake. "What do you think?" George said.

"Could be those two guys," I said, "but it could be anybody."

"Jake didn't seem to have any idea who they were."

"No, he didn't, but he gave us one very good clue. We've got to find this guy with half an ear. Jake might not know him, but somebody at Everleigh does. You don't walk around lounges and brothels in this city with half your ear missing and people not knowing who you are."

"The Everleigh sisters?"

"That's where we'll start. It was in their club. Maybe they'll know the guy or maybe one of the girls who was treated poorly will remember."

"Set for St. Louis?"

"I get there tonight and back sometime tomorrow night."

"Think it will help?"

"Where we stand now is Madeline Marsden taking the full rap while Patricia Farmer gets treated lightly. That doesn't seem right to me." My temples tightened as I thought of the three cases we had and our progress, like walking through thick mud. We needed something to go our way and soon.

• • •

I hadn't seen Joan McDermott in two days and I didn't want her coming by my place while I was on the way to St. Louis so I made a stop at The Bitter End to leave her a note or try and talk with her. I was greeted by Mrs. Flint, the madam. She didn't look very pleased to see me. This may have been due to my last visit where I ruined a room and threatened several of the girls.

"Detective Moses. I am surprised to see you back here so soon," she said. She was an attractive, older woman, tall and thin. Her dark hair was showing a few signs of gray; her face, once pretty, was gathering lines of age.

"I'm sure you got my message that I would pay for any damage that I did during my stay."

She smiled. "The damage probably looked worse than it was. We took care of that."

"I appreciate that," I said.

"Of course, we hope that you will consider us your friend if it ever becomes necessary to have to call the police."

I tipped my hat. "Of course."

"I understand that you have befriended Miss McDermott."

Now I smiled. "We have become friendly."

"She is a good girl, Detective Moses. I would hate for something bad to happen to her."

I knew that she knew what happened to Eleanor Winter. "I will try my very best to protect her in any way that I can."

"Of course," she said.

"I was hoping to talk with her or to leave her a message."

"Oh, maybe I wasn't clear. Joanie isn't here tonight. It's one of her scheduled days off."

I nodded. "That's okay. I just wanted to let her know that I will be in St. Louis tonight and most of tomorrow."

"I can get her that message," she said.

"That would be nice," I said, preparing to leave.

"That awful Captain Garfield was here asking a lot of questions about you after your last visit."

"I'm sure he was. He doesn't seem to like me very much."

"Not only that but he made some terrible accusations, saying that you were dangerous and a murderer. He wanted me to tell him if you ever made a visit here again. He wanted to know if you ever got out of line. He seems like he is looking for any reason at all to get you in trouble."

I spread my arms wide and smiled. "Do I seem like a trouble maker?"

"Most assuredly, but we will say nothing about this visit. Just keep an eye on Joanie and watch yourself. That Garfield is up to something."

"Again, I will do my best."

"And have a wonderful time in St. Louis."

Tracking down information on a manipulating, teen-aged, murderer didn't sound like all that much fun, but I had no options. "Call me if you ever need me, Mrs. Flint." I stepped out of the brothel into August's unrelenting heat and headed for the Illinois Central train station.

• • •

When I returned to Chicago from New York, I didn't recall much of the train ride. Most of this was due to me being extremely hung over. Secondly, I slept for most of the trip. On the ride to St. Louis, I couldn't get comfortable, stayed awake the whole time and watched the sun disappear and the stars come out. By the time we got into the station I was exhausted. At least I was able to get something to eat. When I got to my hotel there was no one in the lobby, but a sleeping clerk. I felt bad waking him, but I had no choice. I needed a room. What had kept me awake on the train was the dizzying lack of information we had on the cases being handled. I couldn't calm myself enough to sleep. Once I got into my room and crawled into the bed this wasn't the case. I fell asleep right away.

Day Seven

I woke early the following day and dressed and got something to eat. I had time before my meeting with Sister Agnes at St. Catherine's Catholic School so I took a walk around. It was easy to spot the first difference between Chicago and St. Louis. Chicago dwarfed the city. Where we had Lake Michigan, St. Louis had the Mississippi. St. Louis also had high humidity, dusty streets and mosquitoes that were bigger than any I'd seen before. I wasn't impressed.

St. Catherine's was a small, two story building that was located on the edge of the town and overlooked a large prairie. When we contacted the school we were told that Sister Agnes was the principal and she would be the one to discuss the school's former student, Patricia Farmer. Before I walked into the building, I thought about stopping into the adjoining church. Was there something in all of this where God could be of help? I stopped before going in. I wondered why God would help me.

A young nun showed me into Sister Agnes' office and sat me down at a chair in front of her desk. She offered me tea, but I declined. She told me she would go get Agnes and return shortly. Behind the desk was a large painting of Jesus. As I looked at it I realized that he wasn't looking at me; he seemed to be looking through me. I shook my head. A picture couldn't look at your soul.

I was still looking up at the picture when a figure entered the room behind me and took a seat at the desk. She stared at me for a moment without speaking. Her face was old, somewhat void of color and she had piercing light blue eyes. Her habit covered her hair. "You are Detective Moses from Chicago?" she said.

"I am, Sister," I said.

"And you came all the way out here to discuss a former student of ours?"

"Yes. Patricia Farmer. She attended school here before her family moved to Chicago."

"I am well aware of Miss Farmer's past association with our school."

Sister Agnes was bringing back memories of how most nuns talked to me at Holy Trinity. They were the boss.

"I am a big fan of mystery novels," Sister Agnes said. "They help me to keep my mind working; they make me think. I particularly like Sherlock Holmes."

I didn't know what to say. "I don't have a lot of time for reading."

"I would imagine that real detective work is not anything like what you read in books."

I laughed. "I think that a good part of my day involves a number of things that no one wants to read about. Another part of it is non-publishable."

"Have you ever had to use your gun?" The good sister was now smiling.

"Once or twice," I said.

"Killed anyone?"

How to answer this? "Yes," I said. Keeping it simple seemed the best course.

Again Agnes was staring at me. Maybe I wasn't what she pictured a Chicago detective to be like. Sometimes I didn't feel like a great sleuth. More like an animal trainer.

"We are only a small school in a growing town," she said. "Last year we had seventy-five students. We might have eighty this year. Enrollment is in a week."

"I see," I said.

"You don't, detective. You don't see. We are such a small school and mostly we deal with quiet children from good families. We don't have much trouble with any of them."

I shifted on my chair. I felt really hot all of a sudden. Was Sister Agnes making me nervous?

"Before I answer any of your questions, I was wondering if I could ask you one."

I cleared my throat and sat up straight. "Of course," I answered.

"What kind of mischief has Miss Farmer gotten herself into in the great city of Chicago?"

There was no reason not to tell her about the case. It wasn't a private matter. "She has been involved in a murder case," I said.

"Murder," she said quietly. "If I had to guess I'm going to say that this murder case wasn't your average, everyday murder."

"No. It was not."

"A few details, if I'm not reaching too far?"

"Patricia Farmer and a friend have been arrested for killing three older women. In no way was this an ordinary murder. Shocking is a good word to describe it."

She smiled thinly. "And torture was involved?"

Now it was my turn to stare at her. She returned it, unblinking. She was starting to unnerve me. "Sister, I don't mean to be rude, and I have no problem with discussing some of this case, but where is this going?"

"This is a small school in a small parish. Like I said, maybe eighty students this year. In such a small group size it's easy to spot someone who is so unique. We have a young student here, Samantha Gibbons. Sweet girl, very quiet. Samantha is an excellent student, but she lacks some social qualities and seems a bit of a loner. She always kept to herself."

I knew where this was going. "Until Patricia Farmer found her?"

Again that little smile. "Ah, you are a detective."

"That's what they pay me for."

"I would assume that you have seen some gruesome cases?"

"There was a killer in Chicago for a while that thought he was doing God's work by removing prostitutes from the streets one at a time. His method of removal was disembowelment."

"Simon Kluge," she said.

"You are a crime fan," I said.

"It was all over the *Dispatch*."

"It was a rather unbelievable case, but let's get back to Patricia Farmer."

"Of course. Would you like some water, Detective? You seem like you are starting to sweat."

I reached up and touched my forehead. It was sprinkled with dots of perspiration. "I would love some water."

She rang a little bell that was sitting on her desk and the young nun who had shown me in came into the office and was told to get us some water. She scurried off in a hurry at the command. "Sister Grace," Agnes said, shaking her head. "Nice young woman, but..." She tapped her head with her finger several times.

"Patricia and Samantha?" I said.

"Well, you said it. Samantha was just going along nice and quiet like and then Patricia found her."

"They became close friends?"

"Too close in my opinion. Samantha was like her little pet, followed her around like you see a puppy follow someone."

I'd heard this before. Patterns were becoming clear. "Somehow Patricia got Samantha to believe that they were best friends?"

Sister Grace returned with a glass of water for me and gave me a friendly smile as she placed it on the desk in front of me. I took a sip and felt better, not as warm.

"Let me tell you a little tale," Sister Agnes said. It amazed me how a nun could always look so cool, wearing the habit in such hot conditions. "Around October, maybe the middle of the month some strange things began to happen around our little parish. I think the first incident occurred out at the Garrett's farm. They woke up on a Sunday morning and found that one of their pigs had been beheaded. The head was gone and found later on top of a cross in the cemetery."

I shifted uneasily and found I was getting warm again. I took another drink of water.

"The second occurrence happened about a week later. This time it was an old dog, a street dog."

"A stray?"

"That's the word I was looking for. He was a little dog, but when they caught him they tied his back feet together and hung him from a tree by them. Then his throat was slit."

"Lastly, we have the Gibbon's cat. His name was Arthur. Arthur was found hanged in a small tree in the back of the Gibbon's house. The family loved that cat and they all cried, even the father."

I played along a bit. "So someone was torturing and killing some of the local pets and animals?"

"You know how this ends, Detective, but that's not the story. The area was becoming a little alarmed. Someone crazy was out there killing local animals. Everyone was a little on edge. The police asked around and came up with nothing. People were waiting for something more to happen, but it didn't. Arthur the cat was the last victim. You want to know why?"

I took a sip of the water. "Enlighten me," I said.

"Samantha Gibbons came to me one day. She looked very distraught. She wanted to know how bad something that you did had to be to go to hell. I asked her what she had done to make her ask such a question. I barely got the question out before she started sobbing. She told me she had killed Arthur the cat. I asked about the other animals and she said she had killed them, too."

"No mention of Patricia?"

"None, but I asked her. I knew they had been inseparable. She actually told me that she had acted on her own. I knew she was lying and I had an idea. I told her to go to the church and go to confession. She left and I went over to wait for Patricia to come into school."

"What was your idea?"

"I was going to tell Patricia that someone had said that she and Samantha had killed the animals. I was going to tell her that Samantha had fessed up already."

"How did Patricia take the story?"

"She didn't. While I was waiting for her I looked in her desk and under some books and paper I found these." She opened her desk and pulled out some drawing paper. She handed them over to me.

There were three pictures in all, a pig, dog and a cat. All were represented in the way they died. All had been sketched in pencil. Every animal face showed the eyes bulging, in horror. At the bottom right of each sketch were the initials, PF.

"I didn't need to confront Patricia," Sister Agnes said. "I had all of the proof I needed. As you detectives say, an open and shut case."

I handed the pictures back. "What did you do?"

"I called in Patricia's parents and showed them the pictures. I said someone had said Patricia had done the killing. Her father didn't take this news that well, but I am the authority at this school. I expelled Patricia. I'm guessing her parents didn't think it was such a good idea to hang around St. Louis so they moved to Chicago. Mr. Farmer still does a lot of business here from what I've heard."

"What about Samantha Gibbons?"

"I called her in and told her I had expelled Patricia. I told her I would not tell her parents and that there was to be none of this in the future or I would expel her as well. I also told her God was watching and she seemed to fear this the most. She has been a model student since this happened."

"You're convinced Patricia got Samantha to do the killing of the animals?"

"One hundred percent. All Patricia did was sketch them after they were dead."

This sounded like our case, but the dead were elderly women. They had been the subjects of Patricia's pictures in Chicago. "If we needed you to come to Chicago for our case, could you?"

"If it would make a difference I would. I would be more than willing to draft up an affidavit of what happened here. I can get it together and mail it to your precinct."

Something struck me as Sister Agnes spoke to me. Suddenly it occurred to me what a total monster we had in Patricia Farmer. She had three times gotten people to do her bidding. The last time it was murder. What would happen if she got a light sentence and was out in a few years? I shuddered as I thought of this.

"Are you okay, Detective? You look a little pale."

"I'm fine," I said. "An affidavit would be an excellent start."

"And you will do your best to see that Patricia Farmer is found guilty in this case and spends a long time in prison?"

I looked closely at her. Those blue eyes were staring at me again. "I will do my utmost best."

"That sounds like a proper ending to a murder mystery."

• • • •

The first train back to Chicago was in the morning so I had plenty of time to kill in St. Louis. I tried my best to behave and to stay away from anything stronger than beer. I found some paper and pencils and drew up everything that I had on Patricia Farmer and the three incidents that she had been involved in. It was clear to me now that she may have never hurt any victims, either animal or human, physically, but she'd had a tremendous amount of influence over the other parties involved in the cases. She was an expert manipulator.

It was my plan that we get together with Jeremiah Higgins, the prosecutor and see what he thought. I thought we should approach Madeline Marsden and her family and lay out what we had found with the other two cases. This might help convince Madeline to break and tell us what had really happened. The other thought was to show Bradley Luke, the Farmer attorney, what we had. If the case avoided trial through plea bargaining, what we had found did not make Patricia look so innocent. If Madeline also told us something that would solidify Patricia as a manipulator that might help.

As I pushed my dinner around on my plate, I tried to reason everything out. This case had my mind in knots. It was probably true that Patricia Farmer never did anything physically to a victim. What was also true was the fact that she was able to persuade three people to do nasty, vicious things for her. This did not make her innocent in my book, but I had no idea what the level of guilt was for her. I would have to leave that to Prosecutor Higgins.

When I returned to my hotel, the same clerk who had been there the night before was on duty. This time he was awake. He told me he had a telegram for me from Chicago. He handed it to me and I stepped over near a gas lamp on the edge of the lobby. It read as follows:

THE EVERLEIGH SISTERS HAVE A GIRL WHO WORKS FOR THEM WHO KNOWS THE ASSOCIATE OF THE MAN WITH HALF AN EAR. NO WORD ON WHO HALF EAR IS. THEY'LL SEE US TOMORROW UPON YOUR RETURN.

LOFTUS

I thought about this for a moment. The only legitimate lead we had were these two men who had heard Allen Price bragging about a safe he had at his home that held a lot of money. One of the men was missing half his ear. Shouldn't be that hard to find him, but then I couldn't find Christian Hanson, a big mute Swede with golden hair that he parted down the middle. We'd see the sisters again and start with what their girl knew.

With Marvin Kell's murder, we currently had nothing. Joey Gulliver and Frederick Munch didn't turn out to be much of a lead. All we still had was a few strands of hair from a black wig and a drunk telling us he saw a police van leaving the scene of the crime. This amounted to zero. I felt bad for Kell. I felt bad for his mother. There were a lot of murders that occurred in the Levee. There were many who we never figured out who killed who. I didn't want Kell, a fellow police officer to be one of those. Right now things weren't looking great.

As well as I slept the night before, this night proved to be the opposite. Patricia Farmer, Allen Price, his family, and Marvin Kell filled my head with thoughts that would not let my body rest. I saw all of the drawings of dead things Patricia Farmer had done. I saw someone in a hideous black wig walk up to Marvin Kell and shoot him in the head. I saw them race away in the police van. Lastly, there were images of someone with a shotgun blasting away at the Price family.

You try sleeping with all of this carnage reenacting itself in your brain. It's the one time where I was sober where I could make a reasonable case for the usage of opium, but not tonight. Tonight I would deal with the demons by myself.

Day Eight

After a long day of travel, I arrived back at the precinct at three o'clock in the afternoon. It would have been easy to grab a bite to eat, a beer and then climb into bed. I was exhausted. I knew that Loftus would be waiting for me; we had to see the Everleigh sisters before they got busy for the evening. We probably had a two hour time frame.

"Did you bring me anything nice from St. Louis?" Loftus asked. He was sitting on the edge of his desk smoking a long cigarette.

"Maybe enough information to sew up our case on Patricia Farmer," I said.

"But nothing particularly for me?"

"Well, I came back."

"Not exactly what I was looking for, but the Farmer news sounds good. You can tell me about it on the way to see the sisters. We've got to hurry a bit."

I explained what I had learned about Patricia Farmer as we walked down Dearborn to the Everleigh Club. We agreed that our next step was to talk with Prosecutor Higgins and decide what to do from there.

"This little girl is as much of an animal as some of the ones she killed," George said.

"Demonic is a good word."

"Christ! What makes people do some of the things they do?"

The normally cold Everleigh sisters gave us more than a warm welcome when we showed up. They actually smiled and told us how happy they were to help the police in such an important matter. We again were sitting in the dining room.

"We are always excited to help the police in any way that we can," Ada said.

"Especially in a case that involves such an awful crime as the murder of the Price family," Minna said.

"We don't know for sure that the men we are asking about were involved in the murders. We heard that they heard a conversation that Price was having rather loudly at one of your faro tables where he bragged about having a large amount of cash in a safe at his home," I answered.

"But that is certainly enough to raise suspicion about them?" Minna asked.

"That's why we are here," I said. "One of your girls knew the man who was with the man with half an ear missing."

"That would be Jenny Fields," Ada said. "Let me get her." Ada rang a little bell and a black servant came into the room. Ada told her to go get Jenny Fields. The servant left as quickly as she had come.

"You look very tired, Detective Moses," Minna said. "Would you like something to eat and drink? We just got a delivery of some great cheeses and we have cold beer. Of course, you too, Detective Loftus."

"Of course," George said. "I'm fine."

"Some cheese and a beer would be great," I said."

"And some sliced ham," Minna said.

"That would be great."

When the servant returned she was followed by a tiny girl, just over five feet tall with long, curly red hair. She looked more like somebody's younger sister than a prostitute. Ada told the servant to go grab my food and drink request; she then told the girl to have a seat. "This is Jenny Fields," Ada said.

"My name is Patrick Moses. I'm a detective with the 22nd precinct. My partner here is George Loftus."

Jenny Fields nodded politely at the both of us, but she said nothing. She looked very shy, a rare commodity in her profession.

"We understand that you may know the man who accompanied the man with half an ear to the club not long ago?" I asked.

"I know him. His name is Billy Baxter.," she spoke quietly, just above a whisper. "He used to have a place over on Wabash. I saw him a lot when I was with The Feline Palace, but not so much recently. I saw him with the man with half an ear, but I didn't say anything to him."

"What about the guy with half his ear missing?"

"I don't know him or his name, but Billy told me that he worked for a man who had half his ear taken off in a knife fight. Billy said the man was a mean one. If you crossed him you could end up dead."

"Did Billy say what kind of work he was in?"

"Horses. Horse racing to be exact. He helped manage Washington Park."

"Was the guy with the half an ear also at Washington?"

"I guess if he was Billy's boss. That would make sense."

Maybe, I thought, but not necessarily. "Anything more that you can tell us about Billy Baxter?"

She giggled. "He was fun to be around, very funny. He was also something of a good lover. He was special."

"Special how?" George asked.

Jenny Fields started to laugh. Tears came out of her eyes.

"I believe, Detectives," Minna said, "that Jenny is trying to tell you that Billy Baxter was rather well endowed."

"So were looking for some punk with a big dick?" Loftus said.

Jenny couldn't stop laughing and she just shrugged at us.

"An address on Wabash?" I said.

Jenny stopped laughing for a moment and wiped her eyes with a handkerchief. "Above Casey's."

I knew where that was. We said are goodbyes just as my food and drink came. I quickly ate a piece of ham and some cheese. I washed it down with two gulps of beer. Loftus helped himself to some of the platter. As we headed out of the dining room door, I heard Jenny Fields and the two sisters start to laugh uproariously. They found the topic of Billy Baxter's manhood rather entertaining.

•   •   •

We got to Casey's just as business was starting to pick up for the evening. The place was a nice, clean gambling parlor. If you were looking for ladies this was not the place. Above the parlor were two apartments. A bartender told us which one Billy Baxter resided in so we made our way upstairs and pounded on the door. There was no answer.

"Probably have to catch him in the morning," George said.

"The races at Washington Park are done for the day. There's no telling when he'll come home. Morning probably is the best time."

We walked back downstairs and stopped at the bar. We were still on duty and not supposed to drink, but I bought Loftus a beer. He didn't object. I was so tired I didn't care if they took my badge from me right there.

When the bartender brought the two beers over I asked him what he knew about Billy Baxter.

"What do I know about him?" he asked.

"Yeah," I said. "What can you tell us about the guy?"

"Billy, he's a nice kid. Always friendly when he stops in here. He's a bit of a ladies man."

"We heard that he works out at Washington Park," I said.

The bartender laughed. "He may spend some time at the track, but he doesn't work there. Anybody that told you he worked there got it wrong. The only time he spends there is to place bets."

"Do you know what he does to make money?" George asked.

"Hey, look, I don't want to get Billy in any trouble."

"We're investigating a murder," I said quietly. "Anything you tell us will be confidential."

He looked around the bar to make sure no one could hear what he told us. "Not really sure, but I hear he helps move some Canadian booze into the city. On a maybe bigger scale, he pushes some dope. Don't know that there is anything wrong with either of those things, but he seems to do pretty well at it. Dresses well and he always has a lot on cash on him."

"You ever see Billy with a guy that's missing half an ear?" I asked.

He thought for a moment. "Can't say I have, but like I said, Billy doesn't really hang out in here. He passes through, says hello, and goes upstairs. I don't know that I've seen him with any men. Women on the other hand, there's been quite a few. Rumor has it…"

"We know," George said, cutting him off. "We heard all about Billy."

The bartender laughed. "Must work. I'm talking good looking ladies."

We were back outside in the heat. George was going back to the precinct for a bit. I was going to head home and try and sleep. I was exhausted.

"We'll see the little boy prosecutor in the morning?" George asked.

"After we stop here," I said.

"What about the Kell case?"

"What about it? Some nut in a wig walks up to Kell and shoots him and runs off in a police van. How many nuts in this city George? Can't question them all."

"We need something else," he said.

"Even the tiniest bit would help us out."

He patted me on the shoulder. "You look beat. You need to get some rest. Something will pop on these cases."

"First two points, I agree. Last one, not so sure."

He patted my arm again and headed towards the 22nd.

Day Nine

I was so tired that I wanted to see no one as night crept into the day. I wanted to see Joan McDermott, but not today. All I wanted was to finally get home and crawl into my bed. When my head did hit the pillow it was only a little after eight and still light outside, but it didn't matter. I was asleep within minutes and was sure to sleep well until morning.

Sometimes things never go your way. I had no idea what time it was when I heard the pounding on my front door. For a fleeting moment I thought it might be Joan. I hoped but I was wrong. When I got out of bed and answered the door there stood George Loftus. He looked as tired as me, but there was also a little sadness in his face.

"Get your damn pants on, Patrick. There's been another cop shooting."

I waited for a moment for this news to register. "What time is it?"

"Just past one. Somebody shot another patrolman at State and 20th."

Loftus followed me into my room where I put the suit back on that I had just taken off five hours before. I noticed that George's clothes, usually meticulous, were wrinkled in many spots. "Same kind of shooting?"

"What I hear it's almost the same. Somebody walked up to this patrolman and shot him at point blank range in the head."

"Well, that clears Joey Gulliver and Frederick Munch."

"We have somebody out there who doesn't care for policemen."

"That could be half the city."

George had a cab waiting for us and the horse drawn took us quickly to the corner of State and 20th. The scene looked similar to the one with Marvin Kell. There were a number of people clumped onto one side of the street. A lot were police officers. This, I figured was where the dead cop was. On the other side of the street was a band of onlookers. Sometimes I wondered if the killer was over there watching to see what he had done play out.

We walked up to the packed crowd and told most of them to get out of the way. As the crowd parted, I could see the feet of the dead cop. The man had enormous feet. I figured he was a very tall man. As we got closer I could see Harold Pinter surveying the dead body. Riley O'Donnell was at Harold's side.

"Same kind of thing as Kell, Harold?" I asked.

"Identical, I'd say," Harold said. "Somebody walked up to this officer and shot him in the head from an extremely close range. The bullet exited the officer's head."

In the light we had, I could see that there was a tremendous amount of blood behind the dead officer's head. The cop was a big man, well over six feet tall. If I was shooting him, I'd be pointing my gun at an upward angle. "Do we have a name for the officer?"

"It's James Bourne, Patrick. He's one of ours," Riley said.

I got closer and looked down at the officer. A good part of his forehead had been blown away by the gun blast, but now I could see that it was Bourne. I'd met him a few times and remembered that he had been a good fellow with a sense of humor.

"He's got a wife and two kids," Riley said.

"Jesus Christ," George said behind me.

"He's not going to help James now," I said. "Anybody see or hear anything?"

Harold looked over at me and righted the glasses on his nose. He looked tired like all of us. "There's a woman inside of Riordan's that saw the whole thing. She was shaking so badly we sent her in there with an officer to have a drink."

George and I turned and headed back through the crowd and into Riordan's, an old bar that had been in the Levee for years. It was odd to enter any kind of drinking establishment at this hour of the day and find it empty, but that's what we found. The place had emptied out to view what had happened to James Bourne. Sitting at the bar was a woman and a uniformed cop. A bartender stood behind the bar, arms crossed over his chest. We walked up to the woman and the cop. "Who do we have here?" I asked.

"Her name is Clara Mitchell," the cop said. "She saw the whole thing. She came over and told us about it and started shaking like a leaf. The funny looking little guy in the glasses told me to take her in here and buy her a whiskey. She wanted another, but I told her she had to wait until after she talked with the detectives."

Clara Mitchell was middle aged, with very straight blonde hair. She was dressed in a simple dress and simple black shoes. She didn't look like a pro, but I wondered why she was up so late. "Clara, can you tell us what you saw happen?"

She was holding her empty whiskey glass tightly. I thought it might snap in her hand. "My apartment is right across the street, second floor. I keep the books at several casinos and I'd just gotten home for the night. I was about to get undressed when I looked out the window. The officer was just walking around the corner, very slowly. I thought how unconcerned he looked."

"Were there other people around?" I asked.

"Sure. Quite a few. People were coming and going, moving in all directions."

"What happened next?"

"Like I said, the officer was coming around the corner when I saw this very tall woman, all dressed in black, approach him. The woman had very dark hair."

"A woman, you say?" George asked.

"A very tall woman," she said. "She walked up to the officer and they talked for a minute. The cop was taller than her. After a moment or two, I saw the woman draw a gun from the folds of her dress and shoot the officer right in the face. The officer fell straight back and I saw the woman walk around the corner as casually as she could. I damn near had a heart attack."

"Then you came downstairs?" I said.

"I couldn't believe it. I hurried outside and walked over to wear the officer was lying. By this time, others were near him. Someone had rung the police. I got a good look at that cop's face. That was when I knew he'd been murdered. That was when I started shaking."

"Get her another whiskey," I said to the bartender. "What more can you tell us about the woman?"

She shook her head. "That's it. Not much. Dark dress and dark hair. Pretty tall I think. Like I said, she walked up to him and they talked for a minute. I never saw the woman's face. Then she drew her gun and shot him. She was around the corner before that cop's head hit the ground."

The bartender gave her the second drink and she took a small swallow. She started to cry a bit. "Worst thing I've ever seen she said."

"Sit with her and walk her home when she is ready," I said to the cop. He nodded as George and I stepped back outside the bar. The coroner's van had shown up to take James Bourne into the morgue. Harold walked over to us.

"Don't know if we'll find any bullet, but I'm thinking larger caliber this time based on the amount of damage to Officer Bourne's forehead. The shot did considerable damage."

I nodded. "Anybody except the lady in Riordan's see anything?"

"Before you got here, Riley had a bunch of cops ask anyone who was standing around that exact question. Nobody came back with any kind of positive answer."

"So we've got a killer wearing a black wig for Marvin Kell and a woman with black hair for James Bourne?" George said.

"Or the same person wearing a wig both times," I said.

George nodded. "Could be, I guess. Where do we start?"

"We've got to talk with everyone in this vicinity and see if anyone saw the killer. We've got enough cops here. Let's see what we can find."

What we found was nothing. We had enough people to check every open business on all sides of the street and up to a block away.

Nobody other than Clara Mitchell saw anything. By the time we were done we were frustrated and beyond exhaustion. I got back home at five in the morning. I was so tired but couldn't sleep. I thought of Soon Lee's, the opium den, but they might be closed. I also thought about myself. I took a step back from the edge. I slept fitfully until eight o'clock. Our meeting with Jeremiah Higgins was at nine at the State's Attorney's office. I would be there on time, but I wasn't sure what kind of shape I'd be in.

We stopped by Billy Baxter's apartment on the way to see Prosecutor Higgins, but there was no sign of the man. George thought that we should break in the place and see what we could find, but I wasn't sure that was a good move. Acquiring evidence in an illegal search might get the case thrown out if we did find something. We agreed to wait and take another stab at Billy later.

Jeremiah Higgins didn't look any older than he had the first time we met him. He still reminded me of someone who was just entering college. Even dressed in a fine suit and expertly tied bow tie he didn't resemble anyone I knew who prosecuted murder cases.

"I trust you gentlemen have found something useful or you wouldn't have called this meeting," he said.

"I hope it is useful," I said, "but I need your opinion first."

Jeremiah got wide eyed. "I thought you said I was too young to be prosecuting anyone."

"But you said we were stuck with you."

He laughed and his stomach shook under his suit vest. "What opinion would you like, Detective Moses?"

"What does it take for someone to be an accessory to a murder?"

Jeremiah sat back in his chair and looked around his plain office. There wasn't much to look at in the office, so I hoped he'd speak soon. "An accessory, to the best of my knowledge, must be helpful in the carrying out of the murder."

"Like providing a weapon that is used to commit the crime?" George asked.

"Exactly," Jeremiah said. "In that case, the accessory has nothing to do with the actual violence, but aided the murderer by giving him the means to kill."

"What about egging someone on to commit the crime?" I asked.

"I don't follow," he said.

"What if you promised someone that you would do something for them if they did something for you? What if you promised to take something away from someone if they didn't commit the crime?" I said.

Jeremiah grabbed a piece of paper and a pencil. "Can you be more specific?"

"In St. Louis, where Patricia Farmer lived prior to coming to Chicago, she befriended a young girl and convinced her that killing some animals would solidify the friendship. The girl went on to kill several animals, including a pet of her own, and a farm animal. She admitted this to a nun who is the principal at her school. The nun was convinced that Patricia would stop being her friend if she didn't carry out the killings. All Patricia did was make pencil drawings of the murdered critters."

"She made pencil drawings?" Jeremiah asked. He was paying strict attention.

"Just like in our case," I said.

"Do you have more than the St. Louis incident?"

"Before attending St. Regina, Patricia went to Abraham Lincoln School on the north side of the city. Again she befriended someone, a boy this time, and promised him a romantic interlude, if he would get another boy to stop bothering her."

Jeremiah smiled. "A romantic interlude? I assume things didn't end well for the other boy?"

"No. The bigger boy pummeled the smaller one and was severely punished. He and Patricia left the school and a financial arrangement was made with the injured boy's family to avoid police intervention."

"And did the bigger boy enjoy the romantic interlude?"

"Never happened. Our Patricia pretended she knew nothing about the matter even though many heard her egg the boy on. She also pretended that she didn't know the abusing boy."

"So no reward of any kind?"

"Nary a kiss."

"So we have this established pattern of Patricia befriending people, getting them to do some nasty things, and then pretending she knows little or did nothing with respect to the wrongdoings."

"That's it exactly," I said. "Just like what we have with Madeline Marsden. The girl in St. Louis sounds like another version of Madeline, shy, a loner. They are very similar except that Patricia convinced Madeline to kill older women, not animals."

"But she went from animals to beating up a boy to killing women. A progression in cases, if you will?" Jeremiah said.

"Looks like that exactly."

"We could get all of these people up here to testify if we go to trial," he said, talking mostly to himself.

"Both the spurned boy in Chicago and the nun in St. Louis would be willing to help if called."

"That's great except that we have Madeline Marsden admitting to the murders. If we go to plea bargaining she would still lose badly and I'm not sure what we could get out of the Farmer side."

"What if we got the Marsden family and lawyer and went and saw Madeline. Tell her what we have found and ask her if that's what happened to her. Get her to realize she's been duped. If she sees it we can run it by Bradley Luke and the Farmer side. Maybe they'll back off their demands that Patricia did nothing and maybe they'll also want to avoid going to trial if we have witnesses to prove Miss Farmer is not so innocent."

Jeremiah rubbed his chubby chin. "I like that, Moses. Let me line something up with the family. If they're okay we can go see Madeline. If that works we'll talk with the Farmer side."

"Any arraignment yet?" George asked.

"I'm holding off. If Madeline says she did it all at the arraignment and Patricia says she did nothing that may cause us issues. Judges sometimes get confused. I don't want him to tell us to nail it down if those admissions come out in a court room."

• • •

The situation in the precinct when we returned was chaotic. There were more people in the inner lobby than I have ever seen. I had barely gotten in the door with George behind me when Sergeant Cooley

130

called out my name. I made my way past an old woman who was crying.

"A couple of your girl friends are here," Cooley said.

My mood for humor was low. "Speak English, Cooley."

"Sergeant Cooley, Moses. Mrs. Kell is holed up in room one; a girl named Joan McDermott is in room two. You can see them first or you can go upstairs and get your ass kicked by Lieutenant Shipley. Oh, and that little scientist wants to see you."

"Mr. Pinter, Cooley."

"Have a nice day, Moses."

I glanced up the stairs to where Shipley would be sitting, seething over no news on the new cop killing. It was much easier to see the two women who waited to see me. Joan was my first choice. "Go upstairs, George, and tell Shipley I'll be right along. Joan is a friend of mine and I can handle Mrs. Kell."

George looked relieved. "No problem. Just don't forget me."

Joan was sitting at a table smoking a cigarette. She looked tired and I was pretty sure she'd come here after a long night. She smiled when I came in the room.

"Miss me?" I said.

"A lot, Patrick, but there's been a problem at the house."

"What kind of problem?"

"Your friend Captain Garfield came to visit last night. He asked for Annie Grimes by name. Annie was available so they went upstairs to one of the rooms."

"I know Annie Grimes?"

"She spent some time with you on your last visit."

My last visit had been fueled by whiskey by the bottle. I don't remember who I saw or talked with. "What happened?"

"Annie is a friend of mine. Garfield asked her what she and you had talked about. She told him that she didn't know anything about you. She said you were there and that you were very drunk. She didn't even recall if you two had spoken."

"That wouldn't be too inaccurate."

"Garfield didn't like what she said and he slapped her around a bit. She may have lost a tooth and she's got a big bruise on the side of her face."

Those few words raised bile in my throat. Did Garfield really expect me, as drunk as I was, to divulge any secrets to a prostitute? "I can come over there and see Annie when I get done here. It may take a little time. What about you? When can I see you again?"

"This is what cops do?" she said. "They hunt down all the shit that lives in the Levee and if they get frustrated or don't get what they want they start taking it out on the innocent ones?"

"Not all cops are like Garfield."

She crushed her cigarette in the ash tray. "I've spent time with you too, Patrick. Is Garfield going to figure that out and come after me?"

"Joan, let's talk about this later. Another cop got shot last night and we are working three cases. We are not getting much help and the brass wants some results."

She stood up and wiped some ash off her dress. "I'm going to stay away for a bit, Patrick. I don't feel very good about this."

I had no idea what to say. I felt like a young boy getting dismissed by his girlfriend. "I'll come by and see Annie as soon as I can get away for a bit."

She started to walk by me out of the room, but stopped to give me a kiss on the cheek. "Watch that Garfield guy. He's gunning for you." She stepped out of the door and closed it behind her.

To say I was in any kind of mood except bad when I went into see Mrs. Kell would have been an understatement. I got myself under control before I entered the room.

Mrs. Kell was seated at the table in this room. She had been crying. On the table near her was a cloth bag.

"Mrs. Kell, are you okay?"

She looked up at me through reddened, tear soaked eyes. She had put on some face powder and it had streaked badly. "We buried my Marvin today," she said.

"I'm sorry to hear that."

"That damn woman who is carrying Marvin's baby didn't even have the decency to attend the funeral. I wish that he'd never met her."

"I know this is not the best time for you."

She wiped at her eyes with her sleeve. I looked for a handkerchief, but I didn't have one. "They tell me that there has been another officer murdered."

"Last night," I said. "Very similar to the way that Marvin was killed."

"You have no idea who is doing this, do you, Detective Moses?"

"I'm sorry. We don't. The murderer last night was a woman or a man dressed as a woman wearing a dark wig. We have a witness who saw this."

She grabbed the cloth bag and reached inside. She withdrew her hand and tossed a clump of black hair across the table. It was a black wig.

"A wig like this?" she said. "Someone hung it on my front door."

I looked down at the wig and the sour taste reappeared in my mouth. "You didn't hear or see anything?"

"I didn't, but I don't have to be a detective to tell you that you are looking for a complete madman."

She was the second woman in the same day who got up from the table and left me standing alone in the room. I took the cloth bag and put the wig in it. I started upstairs for what would be my most fun meeting of the day with Lieutenant Shipley.

Shipley looked like the last time we had seen him, aggravated. The bottle of bromide pills was on his desk; the cap was off of it. His face was a slight shade of red. His eyes appeared more lit up than usual. George and I took seats across the desk from him. I placed the bag with the wig in it at my feet.

"I know you have almost nothing," Shipley said glumly, "but what can you tell me about the shooting last night?"

"A witness told us that she saw a rather big women, with very dark hair walk up to Officer Bourne and shoot him in the head. The woman then turned the corner and calmly walked away," I said.

Shipley belched loudly. "A woman is killing these officers?"

I grabbed the bag at my feet and dumped the wig onto the top of his desk. "Someone, we can assume the killer, put this wig on the front door of Mrs. Kell's house. Mrs. Kell is the mother of Marvin Kell, the first officer shot."

"So a woman is not killing these cops?"

"We don't know who is killing them. We chased motives after Kell was shot, but those fell flat. Now with two murders there is no doubt that someone is just randomly shooting patrol officers."

Shipley burped again. "Suggestions?"

"Maybe two man patrols," George said, "with holsters unbuttoned."

Shipley ran his hands over his face. "And Allen Price?"

"We are looking for two men who overheard Price talking about having a large sum of money stashed in a safe in his house. One of the men is missing half an ear."

Shipley grimaced. "Promising?"

"It's the best thing we have. We know where one of the men lives, but he hasn't been around. There's talk he pushes booze and dope. Once we can contact him we can find the man with half an ear missing."

"And our two little teenaged murderesses?"

"Madeline Marsden still claims she did all the killing; the Farmer girl says she just sat there and drew some pictures. We have found two other case where Miss Farmer coerced people into doing things for her. She has been forced to transfer schools more than once."

"What kind of things?"

"Got a girl in St. Louis to torture and kill animals. Promised a young boy the moon if he would beat up another boy for her. In both cases she claimed she did nothing and knew very little. In St. Louis they found sketches of dead animals that are similar to the ones of the older women."

"What kind of person does these things, Moses?"

"An animal herself."

"What does the prosecutor think?"

"We are going to try and meet with the Marsdens to see if Madeline will change her story based on what we heard. After that, if it goes well, we'll see the Farmer people and see if they want to test going to trial if we can prove all of these things."

"I've changed my thoughts on the convictions. We have to keep that girl off the street at all costs. She may be worse than Kluge," Shipley said.

Simon Kluge had murdered many Chicago prostitutes in his time, using a very sharp knife. Comparing Patricia Farmer to him may have been an exaggeration, but who knew how far she would go.

"I know you are working these cases hard," Shipley said. "I know we are short of people and there is no lack of new dead bodies. Keep working hard, but get me results. I will keep the Central Station and City Hall calm for now, but we've got to put some of these to bed. With that Farmer girl go to the wall to keep her locked up."

•　•　•

Before we headed back out to find Billy Baxter, I told George I needed to see Harold Pinter for a moment. I headed into the basement, past the cell that still held Jake Allard. He was sleeping on his cot and didn't notice me at all. I found Harold working at his desk.

"I brought you a little present."

He looked up as I tossed the wig to him. He caught it and looked at it with wide eyes. "The killer's wig?"

"If you can match those strands of hair you found in the police van."

"I should be able to do that rather simply. I'm trying to get the bullet form Officer Bourne's head but have learned that is impossible. It blew out the back of his head and is somewhere in the street. I went to look earlier, but found nothing."

"If these hair's match up we'll know right away that we have one killer."

He nodded. "I'll get right on that. Oh, by the way, Officer Bourne's hat was missing from the crime scene."

"His hat?"

"We couldn't find it. Maybe a passerby took it."

"Gruesome souvenir."

"Does that surprise you, Patrick?"

I thought for a second. "Not really. How is Martha?"

Harold's eyes saddened. "She is still with us, but she is weak. The doctor doesn't think it will be long."

"Any news from your son?"

"As of today, no. I hope that he will come along before she passes. That is a strong burden to carry with you for your life."

"He'll come," I said.

Harold smiled weakly. "Let me get back to what I was doing. I'll know on your wig and hairs later today."

He went back to work and I headed out of his office and up the stairs to find George. Jake Allard was still asleep.

•　•　•

Casey's was quiet at this time of day, just a couple of lonely boozers at the bar. There was a different bartender than the last time. He paid no attention to us as we headed upstairs in search of Billy Baxter. Again we pounded on his door, but with no answer. For a guy who was known to like a good time, he didn't seem to need much sleep or reason to stay home. Most of the night dwellers in the Levee were easy to find during the day.

There was kid waiting for us when we came downstairs. He was holding a broom in one hand and a cigarette in the other. He might have been fifteen or sixteen; there was little evidence of facial hair. He was wearing tattered clothes and was missing two of his front teeth.

"You with the cops?" he asked.

"What if we are?" George said.

The kid took a puff of his cigarette and blew the smoke towards us. "Billy don't like people sneaking around upstairs, specially no cops. Billy don't talk to no cops."

George looked over at me and then back at the kid. "What's your name?"

"Cyrus. Cyrus Mills. I clean up in here every day. Billy is my friend."

"You don't say," George said. "Why doesn't Billy want anyone sneaking around and why doesn't he talk to cops?"

136

"Says the cops are always trying to fuck with him. Says they ain't good for no business."

"And what exactly does Billy do for business?"

The kid laughed. "I can't tell you that."

Now, I stepped forward. "Listen, Cyrus, we are looking at a case that involves multiple murders. I appreciate the fact that you're Billy's friend, but we need to know where we can find Billy."

He laughed again. "Can't tell you that."

I grabbed Cyrus by the shirt and pulled him in close to me. He dropped his smoke and the broom. "Cyrus, if we find that you know something about Billy's whereabouts I'm going to drag you into the precinct and stick you in a cell and forget about you." Cyrus' eyes were bulging.

"Big fucking rats live down by the cells," George added.

"Leave him alone," the bartender said from behind the bar. "He doesn't know any better and he's not doing anything wrong."

I let Cyrus go. He looked completely flustered. "You ever see Billy with a guy that's missing half of an ear?"

He had started to cry and bit and I felt bad. He was clearly a dimwit. "That would be Mr. Finch."

"What does he do?"

"Something out at Washington Park. I don't know."

"When is Billy around here?"

"Leave him alone," the bartender said again. "Billy just comes in here once in a while. He'll see Cyrus and flip him a dollar. That's it. He doesn't know anything about Billy."

I pushed past Cyrus and up to the bar. The bartender was tall and skinny. His hair was slicked back and he had high cheek bones. He might have had some Indian blood. "Do you know much about Billy?"

"Nothing. He'll stop by the bar and have a beer once in a while. Most of the time he just goes upstairs. Sometimes with a girl."

"What about this Mr. Finch?"

"Don't know anything about a Mr. Finch. I've never seen him and I don't know anything about him."

"Same holds for you. If you're fucking with us, there's a nice spot down in those cells for you."

"That's all I know, Detective, and I've been in cells before. When you're cold and hungry they ain't so bad."

Out on the street, George lit a cigarette. "Seems like we're running in circles."

"The kid's a halfwit. I don't think he knows anything. The bartender seemed to be telling the truth. I think we are just going to have to be lucky to catch up with Billy Baxter."

"What about this Mr. Finch?"

"A trip to Washington Park might be in the cards."

George exhaled a large plume of smoke. "I've got to follow up on an old burglary case. Need me for anything right now?"

"Not this minute. I've got to head over to The Bitter End to check on something."

"You bust up another room?"

"Nothing like that. Somebody hurt one of the girls and I said I would look into it. As a favor for the last time."

He gave me a side eye glance. "You're an interesting fellow, Moses."

I never found myself to be interesting. Confused might be a better word. George headed off down the street and I started for The Bitter End.

•   •   •

Most of the girls who worked The Bitter End were hanging around the bar at this time of day. There weren't any customers that I could see so the girls were not dressed in their finery. Most seemed to be dressed in night clothes and wearing little makeup. I saw Joan talking with some of the girls. She came over when she saw me enter the parlor.

"Mrs. Flint would like to speak with you before you talk with Annie," she said. There was still a coolness to her voice.

"Sure," I said. She turned and led me up a hallway to the back of the house.

Mrs. Flint had a small office that was almost next to the kitchen area. Joan left me there and I knocked on the door. I didn't need to knock twice as the door was opened quickly.

"Ah, Detective Moses, I'm so glad that you could find time to stop by."

I noted a hint of sarcasm, but said nothing. I entered the small office and took a seat in a nice St. Anne's chair. Mrs. Flint sat next to me on a short couch. She was wearing a dark blue dress, buttoned all the way to the neck and black shoes. Her dark hair was tied back; her face showed the time she had put in as a madam.

"I was told that you wanted to speak with me before I saw Annie Grimes."

"I did want to talk with you, but I am not sure you can be of much help."

"What help would you be asking for?"

"I know you were told that Captain Garfield paid a visit and requested to see Annie. After the visit Annie came downstairs and had several bruises on her face. She said that Garfield asked her all about you, but she didn't know much. Then he beat her up."

"I was aware of that. That's why I came to see Annie. What is it that you would like me to help with?"

"It's not good business for a brothel if a police captain shows up, requests the services of one of the girls, doesn't pay and then beats the girl up. If word of this gets out people won't come here and some of the girls might quit."

"I wish I could help you."

Her eyes opened wide. "Can't you talk with him and work out a deal. Perhaps you can give him some of the information he is looking for. Maybe he'll leave us alone."

The kind of information that Garfield wanted from me was not the kind you made a deal over. It was the kind that had you swinging from a noose. "I'll see what I can do about Garfield."

She gave me a small smile. "Annie is in the second room on the right at the top of the stairs."

I don't know if she believed me about Garfield, but I said goodbye and made my way out of the room and to the stairs that led to the bedrooms. The downstairs had been a little lively where the girls were, but the second floor was church like quiet. I found Annie's room and knocked lightly on the door.

"Come in," said a small voice after a short wait.

Annie was lying in the bed with the covers pulled almost up to her neck. Her head was propped up by a couple of pillows. Joan said I had met her, but I couldn't remember. She had bright red hair. She also had a black eye and a cut on her chin. Her lip was cracked on the left side. She wasn't smiling.

"Hello Annie," I said.

"Patrick," she said quietly. Apparently we had reached first name status.

"Can you tell me what happened?"

A single tear rolled out of her eye. "Captain Garfield asked for me and we came up to the room. We had sex and then he asked me a bunch of questions."

"What kind of questions?"

"How well I knew you? How often did I see you? What did I know about your past?"

"What did you tell him?"

"What did I tell him?" she said loudly. "What could I tell him? I've seen you once and you were stone drunk. That's as often as I've seen you. I know nothing about your past."

"I'm sorry," I said. "He seems to think I did something wrong and he's trying to get someone to tell him what they know. I'm sorry he picked you."

Another tear rolled out. "The bastard never paid me, slapped me four or five times and gave me this." She pointed at the bruises and cut on her face. Tightness rolled across the back of my neck and my temples ached.

"Anything you can do to get this bastard?"

I could shoot him, I thought. "I can try and talk to him. See what he's really after."

"That won't help me much."

I said I was sorry again, but now she was sobbing and sniffling. I let myself out of the room and headed downstairs. I saw Joan near the bar and waved her over.

"Is she okay?"

"She may need a friend for a bit."

"I'll go talk with her."

"There is one thing," I said.

Her look was a little of contempt, but maybe she saw my feelings on my face. Her looked softened. "What is it?"

I pulled my pant leg up and undid the knife scabbard I had tied to my calf. The knife was a short, thick, four incher. I handed it to her. "I don't know that he'll come for you, but word make leak that we spent some time together. If he does and he gets rough, don't be afraid to use this."

She looked at the knife for a moment. She seemed confused by my offer. "Do you think he'll want to see me?"

"I only spent a little time with Annie. If he hears we were together he'll come. Don't be afraid to use this."

She took the knife and stared at me for a bit. "Eleanor told me you could be trouble at times."

Trouble, I thought. I had probably gotten Eleanor killed. "Just watch out for yourself."

•   •   •

I remember nothing about how dinner tasted that night. The whiskey I poured into me did nothing to help the burning I already had in my stomach. The aching I had at my temples and at the base of my neck didn't improve. I was not in a good state, but I was cognizant of where I was and where I was supposed to be. All that meant was I was aware of how much booze I drank.

Since we weren't having much luck finding Billy Baxter we were going to try and locate his boss, Mr. Finch, at Washington Park. Since the first race of the day went off at one it was probably a good idea to get there right about then. When it came to the Price murders there wasn't much to go on other than the conversation that Jake Allard heard at the Everleigh Club. So we would track down Finch and then make another stab at Billy Baxter.

Jeremiah Higgins had talked with Madeline Marsden's family and they all agreed that a morning meeting to discuss Patricia Farmer's past was a good idea. Maybe we could all convince Madeline that

Patricia had just used her for all of this and maybe it wasn't such a good idea to take the entire wrap for what had happened. If Madeline didn't come off of her current story there was a good chance she'd get a tough sentence while Patricia could get a much lighter one.

The other two most galling situations in my life, one private and one professional, was why I was drinking whiskey tonight. The murders of Officers Kell and Bourne were perplexing and scary. Someone disguised in a bad, black wig had walked up to these two street patrolmen and shot them in the head. There was no apparent motive other than murder. There were no clues except the wig. Harold had confirmed that the hairs found in the police van after the Kell murder matched the hairs from the wig. We were dealing with one killer. Our only witness to the Kell shooting was a sick drunk who didn't see the actual shooting, but heard and saw the police van leaving the scene. Our witness in the Bourne shooting saw a large woman walk up to the officer and shoot him. She saw the killer walk away and turn the corner. She did not see the killer's face. The use of the wig found on Mrs. Kell's door made us think it was not a woman doing the killing, but we were just guessing. Once in a while cops guessed right. In this case, I had no idea.

As I sipped the whiskey in front of me I considered what to do with Captain Jack Garfield. I could tell him what I knew about the murder of my father and Amos Stokes, but that would land me in prison. That wasn't going to happen. A poor girl like Annie Grimes didn't know anything about me; Joan McDermott knew a little more, but not much. Garfield was going very low and now he was hurting people, people close to me. Joan had decided to part company with me. I had to do something, but what? I really couldn't kill the bastard. My temples and neck tightened. I saw little flashing lights and closed my eyes. I took a deep breath. When I opened my eyes I didn't feel much better, but knew it was time to go. There was too much to do tomorrow to wreck myself tonight.

I stopped at Mercy on the way home. I hoped I didn't smell of booze. My nurse friend was on duty again and she let me upstairs to peek in on Martha Pinter. The room was quiet and hot and smelled of medicine. In the gloom of night I could make out Martha's figure on the bed. There was a very faint sound of her breathing, but it wasn't even. I asked the nurse how much longer she thought Martha could go.

"Only God can answer that question, Detective," she said.

I nodded and turned to go.

"Detective," she said. "Are you alright?"

I smiled. "I'm fine," I said.

"You just look awfully tired."

That was true. I was, but there was little I could do about it. I thanked her and moved out into the August night air.

Trudging up the stairs to my apartment, I looked down as I reached for my keys. When I got to my door I looked up. Hanging from my door was a patrolmen's hat. I didn't have to guess. This was Officer Bourne's missing hat. I took it off the nail it was hanging on and took it into my apartment. I sat in the chair in the living room where Lois Winston had once patched me up. I was able to see the hat better inside the apartment. There was clearly blood splatter under the bill. That didn't unnerve me at all. What bothered me was that I now had an idea who was killing these cops. I also knew why that person was killing the cops. They were being killed to get at me and draw me out. Christian Hanson had reappeared and had upped the stakes. This was a murderous game he was playing and I swallowed hard. I had a feeling that one of us would not survive this round. I wondered for a moment what his next move would be. How many more innocent cops would he go after?

Day Ten

I was glad that I had controlled myself and my whiskey intake the night before. I felt a little groggy, but otherwise okay. This was until I saw Officer Bourne's hat resting on the table where I had left it. Then I suddenly felt nauseous. Christian Hanson, who had killed Gunter Krause and Sam Walker was back. Hanson had terrified little Freddie Winston, trying to get at me. He had tortured girls in a Blue Island farm house, attempting to make them prostitutes. He was evil, the devil himself. I would turn the hat over to Harold, but I needed to let George Loftus know that Hanson was back. It might help if everyone knew the madman was around. It would keep you alert. Maybe you could get the draw on him.

I grabbed Harold and George and we made our way up to Shipley's office. The lieutenant looked better today. At least he wasn't belching and grimacing with pain in his stomach. I placed the hat on his desk.

Shipley looked at the hat and said nothing for a minute. He flipped it over and spotted the same blood stains I has seen. "Where did you find it?" he asked.

"I didn't find it. It was hanging from a nail on my apartment door," I said.

"I suppose you know who put it there." He reached for his bottle of bromide.

"No doubt. The man we are after is Christian Hanson, a murderous fiend."

Shipley nodded. I knew he knew who Hanson was. "And how do we find Hanson?"

"He's a big son of a bitch. Blonde hair, parts it down the middle. He's also a mute."

"That's pretty descriptive. He shouldn't be that hard to find."

I laughed. "When he wants to be he's easy to spot. When he hides it's like he goes into hibernation, like he lives in a cave."

Now Shipley rubbed his tummy. "What do we do?"

"He's definitely trying to draw me out. It's another game for him, but a dangerous one. I'd double the patrol units. I don't know where he is so he could strike anywhere."

He nodded. "Moses, you don't know anyone who knows this man?"

"I do. He's done some work for Big Jim Colosimo. Colosimo last told me he had no idea where he was, but I can ask again."

Shipley just nodded again. "Get me something soon. I'm not sure City Hall, Central Station or my stomach will wait much longer before something breaks."

I looked back at the lieutenant before we left his office. He was popping a number of bromide pills into his mouth.

Harold, with Bourne's hat in his hand went downstairs to his lab. George stood by my desk and lit a cigarette. "What do you want me to do about Hanson?"

His face looked tense as he took a drag off the smoke. "Stay alert. He's after me and it might not be to kill me. He likes to torture people and torment me. He would not be a good one to try and talk things out with. If you see him, kill him. We will figure out the cover for what happens, regardless of how things go down."

George nodded. "And Colosimo?"

"I'll handle him myself. We have history together. It's not all good, but he may feel he owes me a little something."

"The meeting with Higgins is at eleven. After that Washington Park."

"We'll leave shortly."

I watched George walk the short distance to his desk and sit down. His back was to me. He might have had the same worries I did about the Levee. Now he had the thought of Christian Hanson roaming about, looking to kill cops and maybe anyone close to me.

•   •   •

The scene in the small room was already a glum one when George and I arrived. The Marsdens, Sally and Richard, were there with their attorney, a short, serious looking soul by the name of Baldwin. Prosecutor Jeremiah Higgins was present and was thumbing through papers he had spread out on the table. George and I sat down on his side of the table. He waited until we were seated before he spoke.

"As you are well aware, Mr. and Mrs. Marsden, Madeline has taken full responsibility for killing the three older women in this case," he said.

The Marsdens look petrified. Poor Sally was clutching tight to a handkerchief. They both gave Higgins a slow nod.

"Our reasoning for this meeting is to show Madeline what the detectives have found out about Patricia Farmer during their investigations. Based on what they have discovered, we feel that we may be able to get Madeline to change her story a bit and not take the full blame for the murders. If we can convince Madeline to help us there is a chance that we can talk to the judge and maybe he will reduce her sentence."

Sally Marsden made an audible gasp. "The judge won't execute her?" she asked.

Jeremiah managed a small smile. "No Mrs. Marsden. I would think Madeline will spend time in the Children's Home until she reaches an adult age and then be transferred to the county jail. It's all up to the judge, but just so you are not surprised, this is a capital case. I don't think the judge will be overly lenient."

Sally started to cry a bit and then there were a few sobs. Richard tried to take her hand, but she pushed it away. He looked over at us. "What kind of sentence is Patricia Farmer facing?"

"Hard to say," Jeremiah said. "Madeline has said publicly that she committed all of the physical acts on the deceased women. She has said that Patricia did nothing physical to the women. We know she drew the damning pictures. If that story holds and Madeline doesn't change I don't know what the judge will do to Patricia.'

Richard nodded. He looked over at George and me. "You believe you have some information that will help sway Madeline's opinion of what happened?"

I cleared my throat. "We have some knowledge of past incidents involving Patricia. They are similar in nature. Patricia has a habit of conning people into doing evil things for her. We believe that this is what happened with Madeline. We hope she'll see that and come around on her admissions."

"She made Madeline do these things?" Sally said loudly.

"We think she threatened her friendship with Madeline if Madeline wouldn't do some of these things."

Richard shook his head; Sally went into another crying fit. The door opened and the same matron led Madeline into the room. She still wore the same baggy, gray dress. Her hair looked unclean, and gnarled. There were dark circles underneath her eyes. Her looks caused Sally to convulse even further. Madeline plopped into the open chair and stared hard at the table, not acknowledging her parents. The matron left the room without giving us a timeline.

"Madeline," Lawyer Baldwin said, "these detectives are here to try and help you. Prosecutor Higgins is also on your side although he works for the state. You have admitted sole responsibility in the murders of the three women. This will draw a harsh sentence from the judge. The detectives and the prosecutors want to present some evidence to you that may help in your overall sentencing."

I liked what Baldwin had said. It made us all look like we were trying to be friends, which we were. Madeline was not so impressed. She didn't acknowledge any of it, continuing to look at the hard wooden table top.

"Miss Marsden," Jeremiah said, "I want you to pay attention to what the detectives have to say. I believe they have some information which might make you change your mind about what happened leading up to the murders."

"It won't," Madeline said dryly.

"Madeline," Sally said. Her eyes were red and soaked. "Please look at me."

Madeline finally looked up and seeing what state her mother was in, I saw a flicker in her eyes and a look of sadness.

"These people are all here to try and help you. Please listen to what they have to say," Sally said.

"I'll listen," Madeline said quietly.

"Detective Moses, will you present your findings?" Jeremiah said.

As my name was announced, Madeline glowered at me. I wondered if my powers of persuasion could outperform her obvious dislike of me.

"Madeline," I started, "I am going to tell you two stories about Patricia that happened before you even met her."

Madeline's eyes returned to the table.

"Before Patricia moved here she lived in St. Louis. While there she befriended a classmate. In return for a promise of a continued friendship, she convinced this other girl to do some awful things. The other girl killed a pig, a dog and her own family cat. Due to this other girl's guilt she went to a nun at her school and confessed what she had done. She told the nun that Patricia said she would still be her friend if she did these things. When Patricia was confronted by this she denied everything. She said she didn't know anything at all about what the other girl was talking about. This might have been believable, but the nun found several drawings that Patricia had done. They were all drawings of the murdered animals."

Madeline's head popped up and there was a hint of understanding in her eyes. It was only momentary.

"Patricia was asked to leave that school and her family moved to Chicago where she attended Abraham Lincoln School on the north side. It was at this school where she met a young boy in her grade. She made him promises of friendship and maybe romance if he did a small favor for her. There was another boy who was pestering her so Patricia asked the second boy if he could get the first boy to leave her alone.

The young man, smitten by the promises of loves, beat the other boy up badly. The second boy was asked to leave by the school; Patricia, even though many other children heard of her involvement, denied that she knew anything at all about the caper. The school asked her to leave as well. The police were not called in, but both Patricia's family and the second boy's reached a financial settlement with the injured boy. The boy that did the bidding for Patricia said she never spoke to him again after the nasty deed was done. She pretended that she didn't know him. It was at this point that Patricia transferred to St. Regina."

"Do you see where Detective Moses is taking you here, Madeline?" Jeremiah Higgins asked.

She turned towards the boyish looking prosecutor, but said nothing.

"Do you see any familiarities in the cases he explained to your case?" Jeremiah said.

She said nothing and her eyes returned to the table.

"Please answer the gentlemen, Maddy," he father said.

"I see nothing like that," she said.

"Madeline," Lawyer Baldwin said, "the prosecutor and the detectives are here to try and help you with the solution to this case. By helping them, they can try and get your possible sentence reduced."

"Please, Maddy," her mother pleaded. "Please listen to these men and tell them the truth."

There was nothing but silence from the teen killer.

"Madeline," Baldwin said, "did Patricia Farmer promise you that she would continue to be your friend if you killed the women or did she say to you that she would stop being your friend if you didn't kill them? Did she ever make any kind of a threat or an offer like that?"

This was the key question to prove how much control Patricia had over Madeline. If her threats of continued friendship proved how much she could manipulate Madeline we could possibly show this to the judge or work out a deal with Farmer's defense team.

Madeline raised her eyes to face the whole group. She didn't look nervous or scared. She showed no signs of tension. "I know what you are trying to do. You are trying to get me to admit that Patty had as much to do with the actual murders as I did. I'll never say that because it is not true. I'll also never say that Patty said she wouldn't be my friend if this or that didn't happen because that is not true. I killed those women. Patty drew some pictures. There is absolutely nothing more that I will say."

Madeline Marsden got out of her chair and opened the door before the matron could even get to it. No one had a chance to say a word before they were both out of the room.

Sally Marsden burst into tears and was comforted by her husband.

"Fuck. What was that?" George said.

"That went well," Jeremiah Higgins said.

For my own thoughts, I guess was I was more than shocked. It was clear that Patricia had complete control of Madeline. I could never have imagined the depth of it.

"Let me give this matter some thought," Jeremiah said. "I'll contact you shortly as to how we should proceed, but this will require my complete attention. If we go to Lawyer Luke with this he will laugh in our face."

George and I both found us nodding our heads in agreement. This level of legal thinking was way above our pay grade.

• • •

We grabbed a carriage to take us on the ride to Washington Park. It was shortly before one o'clock and the first race would be going off soon. We made a quick stop to check on Billy Baxter, but he didn't answer his apartment door and the bartender, the third one we met, hadn't seen him at all. Billy was fast becoming one of the hardest people in the city to find.

Between the stop to see Billy and the long ride to the racetrack there was little conversation between Loftus and me. What was there to say? Our ploy to get Madeline Marsden to help us get a greater sentence for Patricia Farmer had gained nothing. It looked like Madeline would take the fall and Patricia might get off rather easily. It seemed improbable, but likely.

As we entered Washington Park there was a roar from the crowd, a rising crescendo. It was obvious that the first race was coming to a conclusion. It was a good time to see if we could find Mr. Finch before the next race started.

"How are we going to find this guy?" George asked.

"We'll ask someone of importance," I said. "Finch sounds like some sort of big shot. He probably hangs around in the expensive boxes."

It was another unbearably hot August date and the size of the afternoon crowd surprised even me, but people loved to gamble on the horses and this was the spot. We made our way up to the more expensive box seats, those covered from the sun, and were stopped by a guard at the entrance. We flashed our badges. He smiled.

"What can I do you for you guys?' he asked.

"We're looking for a guy named Finch," I said. "Only thing I can tell you about him is that he is missing half on an ear."

"That would be Rupert Finch. Sits in a box on the finish line, first row. Can't miss him. Wears a bowler hat all the time. Also only guy in here with half an ear."

We made our way towards the center of the track and followed the stairs down to the boxes where the more affluent hung out. These boxes were not as crowded as the general admission seats where the less fortunate were trying to hit something big. It wasn't hard to spot Finch. He was in the first row, no suit jacket, but the bowler perched on his head. We moved into the row behind him and sat down. He didn't notice us as he was looking intently at a racing sheet.

I reached around him and flashed by badge in his face. "Rupert Finch?" I asked.

He didn't turn. "Just Finch," he said. "I have never liked my first name."

"Okay, Finch. We'd like to ask you a few questions."

I was on the side of him where I could see the half ear. The top part had been removed and it hadn't been a clean cut. What was left of the ear showed a jagged edge. I also saw the muscles in his neck tighten. "You can come and see me in the morning in my office," he said.

"Right now I'm concentrating on the races. I have a stake in a couple of three year olds today."

His arrogance caused my own neck to tighten and I heard George moan. "I think now would be a better time," I said. "We can do it right here; you can still watch your horses. Or we can drag you to the Twenty Second and ruin your day."

He made a pencil note on the racing form. "Go ahead and ask your questions."

"You know a guy named Allen Price?"

He seemed to think for a moment. "Can't say that I do. Should I?'

"Allen and his family were murdered over a week ago. During our investigation your name and that of Billy Baxter came up."

"A murder? I wouldn't know anything about a murder. Why did someone murder this Price and his family?"

"That's what we are trying to figure out. What about Billy Baxter?"

Flint laughed. "I know Billy. Fancies himself as a playboy, but he is really a bit of a dolt."

"But he works for you?"

"Billy has done some work for me. That is true, but I don't think he is capable of murder. He might break a few hearts here and there, but not murder."

The horses were getting into their gates, getting ready for the start of the second race.

"What kind of work are you engaged in, Mr. Finch?"

From the side I saw him smile. "Commerce," he said.

"You can't be a little more forthcoming than that?"

"My lawyer, Jay Johnson, will be happy to answer all of your questions regarding my business activities so unless you have further questions or a reason to detain me I'd like to get back to my races."

With that George swung his hand and sent the nice bowler Finch was wearing sailing across several seats. Finch turned to face us for the first time, anger showing clearly. To match the missing piece of his ear was a nice scar running along the top of his forehead that run all the way to the middle of his head. His scarce hair couldn't hide it, the reason for the bowler.

"You've made a big mistake, Detective," he said.

"Shut up," I answered, "or into the precinct in cuffs it will be."

He wore the scowl and a red face. "What do you want?"

"Never heard of Price?"

"Never."

"You weren't in the Everleigh Club recently and overheard Price boasting about a large sum of money that he had in a safe in his home?"

"I was recently in the Everleigh Club, but I have no idea what you are talking about?"

"Where were you in the evening hours last Sunday night?"

The second race started and Finch returned his gaze to the track for a moment. We all watched as the horses raced around the dusty oval. I had never been a horse guy. There was too much information that you had to know before you would put money on an animal. I didn't have the time or patience to gather that information. To the roar of the crowd, the race ended. Finch made a few notes on the racing form.

"Sunday night? Dinner at The Bankers Club in the loop until about nine and then home with my lovely Catherine. Woke up the next day with my arms around her. You can ask her. She's a very nice girl and never lies."

I didn't like this guy, but I had the feeling what he said was the truth. He also didn't seem like the cold blooded, murdering type, but that didn't mean he wasn't involved. There wasn't much more to say. "We'll be in touch," I said.

"I look forward to it," he said.

"Another in a long line of assholes that we get to deal with on a daily basis," George said as we left the track.

"Sure is a pompous one."

"Clean, you think?"

"Maybe, but I don't think we should give up on him."

"Seems like somebody else didn't care for him with the cut off ear and the scar on his head. Must have been a sharp knife."

"Sometimes an attitude like that will draw an unfavorable reaction."

"Like to hear the story, though."

"Let's figure out this story first."

•   •   •

Jim Colosimo was on the gambling floor of the Paris casino when I arrived. His secretary led me to his office and told me to have a seat while she went and found him. I sat in one of the plush seats facing the huge mahogany desk and suddenly felt very tired. I closed my eyes for a second and thought of just falling asleep. The muscles in my neck loosened. The first thing I saw when I opened my eyes was the decanter of whiskey that sat on a table behind the desk. There were four glasses beside it. I knew this whiskey was for Jim's important guests or friends. I was neither of these, but I got up from my chair and went to the bottle. I removed the cork and smelled the whiskey. It was good stuff. I poured two fingers in one of the glasses and replaced the cork. I lifted the glass to my lips as the office door was opened and Colosimo entered the office.

"Help yourself, Moses," he said after seeing what I was doing. He moved towards his desk and I went back to my chair. "It's a single malt from Scotland, somewhat expensive."

"It's very smooth," I said.

"I'm glad you're enjoying it," he said, "but for some reason I don't think that you came to my office to sample my scotch."

I took another sip of the scotch. As usual, Colosimo was dressed in a white suit. The summer had made his skin a golden brown. The gold rings on his fingers still shined. "You've heard about the two police officers who were gunned down while walking their beat?"

"It was all over the papers. It wasn't exactly a secret."

"I know that." I took a sip of the whiskey. I could have drank the whole decanter. "I know who's doing the killing."

Colosimo raised his eyebrows. "Maybe you should go arrest them instead of sitting here drinking my booze."

"I would if I could find them."

He laughed. "Not always easy to find who you are looking for. By the way, I noticed you are here without your partner. He didn't meet his demise, did he?"

I smiled. "Detective Loftus is doing quite well."

"So if you know who is committing these awful murders why are you here with me?"

I sat up straight. "Because I think you can find him for me."

Now Big Jim poured himself some whiskey and took a sip. "Who are you looking for, Moses?"

"An old friend of yours, Christian Hanson."

"Hanson! I haven't seen Hanson in months. I told you the last time that we talked about him that I had stopped using his services, that he was too dangerous. That hasn't changed."

"So you don't know where he is?"

"I don't."

"But you could find him if you really needed him for something?"

He eyed me over the top of the whiskey glass. "You think Hanson is behind these murders?"

"I don't think he's behind them. I think he did them."

"That's a strong accusation."

"Killing police officers on the street is not good for anyone, because if it happens again, we are close to the department tearing the Levee apart to find anyone or anything that helps us find the killer."

Colosimo mulled this for a moment. "What makes you think I can find him?"

"Mr. Colosimo, I know your status in the Levee and the city. I know if you want to, you can find whoever you are looking for."

He nodded, taking in the compliment. "And why should I help you, Moses?"

"Because we are friends?"

He laughed loudly. "That's very funny. Give me one more reason."

I sipped again. "I will owe you one." I hated myself as soon as I said it, but I had to find this bastard.

"That might be a tradeoff. Let me see what I can find."

My glass was empty. I held it up, but Colosimo shook his head. "Do you know a smug prick named Finch?"

"You trying to find him, too?"

"No. I know where he is. Just trying to figure out what he's up to."

"You are right, Moses. He is a smug prick and I don't like him. I hear he moves illegal booze, Canadian I think, and dope. He's a big horse player."

"That's the guy."

"What did he do?"

"Not sure yet, but I'm not getting a good feeling."

"I hear he would kill his own mother for a hundred bucks."

That remark caught me off guard. I was sure that if Allen Price bragged about money in a safe at his house it was more than a hundred dollars. Maybe Finch had no problem killing anyone for money.

•   •   •   •

After dinner, I found myself walking through the Levee. The air had cooled and the moon was hidden by thick clouds. I had behaved myself at dinner. A meeting was set in the morning with Jeremiah Higgins to set our course for the next plan of action. Madeline Marsden's refusal to say that Patricia Farmer had anything to do with the murders was maddening and self- destructive. It was getting late and maybe all we could get was a stiff sentence for Madeline and a softer one for Patricia. There didn't seem to be much more that we could do.

I stopped in front of the Bitter End and looked up at the second floor where I knew the girls would be busy at this time of day. I didn't know if Joan was up there with someone or even if she was in the house. I worried about Jack Garfield and what he would do in his quest for information about me. I had seen what he had done to Annie Grimes. I hoped he would leave the other girls alone, but I wasn't sure of anything.

When I got to Soon Lee's the temptation to go into the downstairs opium den almost got me. I felt tense and a little sweat appeared on my forehead. I could almost feel the pipe going into my mouth; I could almost taste the bitter opiate. I stopped short of going in. The blood splattered bodies of the Price family intervened and got me to stop. I thought Rupert Finch was a sneaky crook, but that was a far cry from being a murderer. His alibi for Sunday would probably hold up. If it did, what did we have? Nothing. I turned and walked up the street.

As I got to my building, I felt my neck tighten and my temples flared. Thoughts of Hanson roaming through your building would do that. He had once kidnapped Freddie Winston and had murdered my landlord in cold blood. He nailed Officer Bourne's hat to my door. I had to find him and fast. I knew Colosimo could help me, but how quickly he moved was the unknown. Hanson had murdered two officers to get my attention. I had to stop him. I drew my gun and made my way up the stairs to the second floor. There was nothing on my door. I unlocked the door and pushed it open. Nothing. I let out a deep breath. It seemed that, at least for this night, I would be left alone. That didn't mean that I would go to sleep with my revolver far from me. I wasn't that relaxed.

Day Eleven

Even with his young, cherubic face, Jeremiah Higgins looked older and tired when we met him the following morning. He had decided to come into the precinct so that we could talk freely, away from any interruptions. We were in one of the meeting rooms on the first floor. He had brought his case file with him, but it was unopened in front of him on the table. I had slept pretty well and was eager to hear what he had to say; Loftus complained of a toothache and it looked like he didn't want to be there at all.

"Obviously, this is a most distressing case," Jeremiah said. "We have two murderers. There is no disputing that, but we have one that is accepting all of the blame for actually doing the killing. Madeline Marsden refuses to implicate Patricia Farmer with anything other than sitting there and drawing pictures. It's disturbing the control that she is under. She is going to get a heavy sentence; Patricia much lighter."

"What can we do? The Marsden girl doesn't look like she is going to move off of her stance," I said.

"In discussions with this lawyer Luke who is representing Farmer, he insists that she did nothing physical to any of the women. He claims that his client was a bit of an innocent bystander to the crime. He paints Marsden as the animal here. He claims Farmer was under her spell, just the opposite of the truth. He's going to ask the judge for some leniency in sentencing."

"What does the state want?"

Jeremiah laughed. "Maximum we can get for both. Madeline Marsden is going to get that. With Farmer, she gets a light sentence, gets out in several years, and goes back to what she was doing before. That is what I'm trying to stop."

I looked over at George. He had a finger deep in his mouth, probing at the aching tooth. "I don't see that there's a lot more that we can do on our end. I'm not sure what more dirt we can find on Patricia Farmer."

"That's true. That is why I'm proposing that we reject the plea offer from Luke. We're going to meet with him and lay out our case of why we think that the Farmer girl is just as guilty as Madeline Marsden. We'll make him go to a trial and let the jury decide."

"And you think that might work?"

"Of course. We bring in the nun from St. Louis, the kid from the north side, we can't lose. The jury hears how Patricia manipulated these people there's no way they don't see her as evil."

I had to agree. We were hardened detectives. What we had learned about Patricia Farmer had stunned us. "That sounds like a good plan."

"Let me set up the meeting with Bradley Luke. I'm going to hit him hard and I'll need you there to hammer away at what we've found in the most negative way. Once he hears the evidence, he won't want to face a trial and he'll have to change his plea. That will up our chances of a stiffer sentence."

Jeremiah nodded as he said this. I nodded, too. George, if he was paying any attention, was still playing with his bad tooth.

•　•　•

We had no sooner stepped out of the meeting room when Sergeant Cooley summoned me over to the front desk. He looked a little frantic. "There's been a murder over a Casey's. Riley and Pinter are already headed over there. They told me to tell you and Loftus to get there as soon as you could."

"Stop playing with your damn tooth. We've got to get going," I said to George.

"Sorry, but it's killing me. What's up?"

"There's been a murder over at Casey's. Riley and Harold are on their way over there."

"Casey's? Couldn't be Billy Baxter?"

"Could be," I said.

There was a carriage in front of the precinct building so we hopped in and told the driver to get us to Casey's. As soon as we left the precinct, we found ourselves stuck behind a broken down milk truck. We considered jumping out and walking, but the driver got around the truck and had us going in the right direction. When we got to Casey's the place was crawling with people, mostly cops. They were trying to keep the people away from the bar and the alley that ran alongside of it. When we stepped out of the carriage, I realized how hot it was.

There was a slight logjam as we worked our way through the mass of people on the outside of the tavern. We badged ourselves past the cop guarding the door. Inside wasn't much better. There were a number of uniformed cops inside, a few patrons were still straggling.

"Get those damn people out of here," I said to one of the uniforms. "What's going on here?"

"Detective O'Donnell and Mr. Pinter are upstairs," the cop said.

We got to the staircase and got up them as fast as we could. The door to Billy Baxter's apartment was open. A big cop stood to the side of it and waved us in. In the main room it looked like everything was pretty normal. We made are way into the bedroom. Harold was busy looking over a partially clad body on the bed. Riley was busy writing something on a piece of paper.

"Is that the elusive Billy Baxter?" I asked.

"We think so," Riley said.

George and I stepped closer and I could see what Riley meant. The man in the bed had been beaten badly. It was obvious that most of the body had taken blows, but especially around the head and upper body. There was bruising from the chest up. The head, what was left of it, looked like a squashed melon.

"Jesus Christ," George said. He seemed to have forgotten his tooth.

Harold looked up at us. His glasses had slid down to the end of his nose. "Nasty business here, Patrick. Whoever got to this fellow beat him to death. I'd say wooden clubs were the weapon of choice."

"Is it Billy Baxter?"

"I think so. It's his apartment."

The headboard behind Billy's head was covered with blood and other bits of his head. All of the sheets were soaked in blood. "Who called it in?"

"The maid went up to clean the room like she always does and the door was open," Riley said. "She entered the apartment and walked into this room. She found Billy and she screamed. The bartender is the one who called the precinct."

"Any idea how long he's been here, Harold?"

"What is it now, around eleven? I'd say six or seven hours based on the rigor in the body, but I'm not sure."

"Anything seem to be missing?" George asked.

"Didn't bother to look," Riley said. "Whoever killed Billy came here to do just that. They weren't trying to rob him."

"Here's something," Harold said. "Take a look."

I walked around to the side of the bed that Harold was on and looked at what he was pointing at. In Billy's left hand, in a death grip, was a one shot Derringer. With a cloth in his hand, Harold reached down and pried the gun from Billy's fingers. He lifted it to his nose and smelled it.

"It's been recently fired," he said.

He handed the small gun to me and I checked the chamber. It was empty. It looked like Billy got off one shot. George, Riley and I checked all of the walls in the direction that Billy could have fired. We didn't find any bullet holes.

"Maybe he hit one of the son of a bitches," George said.

"We can check Mercy for a gunshot wound," Riley said.

"Doubt they'd go there," I said. "Let's go downstairs and see what anybody knows, George. Riley, stick with Harold."

We made our way downstairs and I saw the bartender we had dealt with on our first trip here. He looked as tense as everyone else.

"You called the precinct?" I asked.

"I did," he said. "We heard Becky screaming and I ran upstairs. I thought she was going to have a heart attack. She had just come on for her shift. I helped her downstairs and sent her home. Then I called the precinct."

"Nobody you're aware of heard or saw anything before the maid that went upstairs?" I asked.

"Not that I know of. I came on at eight. Becky went up there at a little past ten-thirty. She said the door was open and she walked right in. Then she yelled. Before us nobody heard or saw anything."

There was a commotion by the side door that led out to the alley. A big cop named Jeffries came through the door and straight over to us. "You'd better come see this, detectives," he said.

We followed him through the side door into the alley. The sun was peaking now and it was hot. The bartender had followed us out of the bar. We followed Jeffries over to where some trash bins were located. A number of uniforms were mingling about. They separated when they saw us coming. Wedged between the two bins was a small body, lying on his back, looking straight up at the sun. I got closer and peered at the face.

"It's that kid, Cyrus," I said.

"Billy Baxter's friend?"

"That's the one." I looked closer and I could see the neat cut above the Adam's apple. Somebody had slit his throat from ear to ear. All the blood had run out the side of the wounds and around his head. There wasn't much on the front of his clothes.

"Somebody didn't like the smart talk he gave out," George said.

"He was just a stupid kid. They probably asked him if Billy was around and he got wise with them and they shut him up."

"Who is they?"

"Somebody Finch knows, I'm thinking," I said. "We gotta get the coroner over here to get him out of this alley."

"Jesus," the bartender said when he saw Cyrus. "He was just a dumb old kid."

"Think Harold will want to look at him before they come with the van to get the body?" George asked.

"Let's find out and then let's go see Mr. Finch."

We walked back into the bar, leaving some uniforms to watch Cyrus' body. Another cop grabbed us and said the lady at the bar wanted to talk to us. He said she said it was important. I looked at George and he shrugged. He walked over to the bar.

The woman sitting at the bar had an ashen face. This was undoubtedly due to the news of Billy Baxter's murder. She was a younger woman and not unattractive. She might have been more attractive if not for her mental state.

"My name is Detective Moses," I said. "The officer said that you wanted to speak with us." I noticed that her hands were shaking.

She looked up at me and I thought she might start crying. "I saw them. I saw the two who killed Billy."

"Where did you see them?"

"I was with Billy. We were friends," she said, smiling shyly. "I liked him. He was fun."

She still looked very nervous. "What's your name?"

"Vera. Vera Whitlock. I just came downstairs. I had been sleeping when I heard all the noise."

I took hold of her hand. I could feel the tremble. "Vera, it's very important that you tell us exactly what you saw. We want to track these people down as quickly as we can."

She nodded. "I was leaving Billy's place. It was about three in the morning. I live right down the hall from him. Like I said, we were friends."

"We got that part. Tell us what you saw."

"I was just about to go in my apartment when I turned and saw them coming up the stairs and into the hallway. I'd seen them before. They had been with Billy a few times. I remembered them because I didn't like the way the one man looked."

"How did he look?"

"Bald head and a thick, black beard. He looked evil. He also had these beady, black eyes. They always looked like they were looking through you."

"You met them?" I asked.

"One time. Billy introduced us all by the bar. I didn't like them."

"So what happened?"

"I was going in my apartment. They were coming up the stairs towards Billy's. Other than the late hour, I didn't think much about it. I never thought something like this would happen." Her hand trembled more.

"If you met them, do you remember their names?"

"Just the one with the beard. Arnold Perry. Billy told me that both of the men worked out at the Stockyards and lived in the last house on Halsted before you got to the yards, an old yellow house. Billy said he had to go there once. He said he didn't like them, but they did odd jobs for him now and then."

I nodded. "What exactly did Billy do?"

"Worked for a man named Finch, but that's all I know." She started to cry a bit and I handed her a handkerchief I had in my pocket. She didn't let go of my other hand.

"You sure these were the guys you saw last night?"

"Yes, detective. I wasn't drinking and I saw them clearly. It was them."

"And you're sure about the name of the one?"

"No doubt. The man scared me. He reminded me so much of an old drawing I had seen of Satan. When I met him at the bar I thought I was actually talking with the devil."

There was no doubt that we had to find this house by the yards and see if the two men were there. We went back upstairs to where Harold was finishing up with Billy Baxter. Riley was outside of the apartment.

"I can't be in there anymore," he said. "That's one of the worst I've seen."

I patted Riley on the shoulder and went in to see Harold. He was putting things in his bag. "You all done?"

"I am, Patrick. Unfortunately, no real clues that can help us other than the gun he shot."

"Well, there's another victim in the alley. A poor, dumb kid named Cyrus. I'm pretty sure the guys who did Billy also killed Cyrus. Cut his throat. I thought you might want to take a look before the coroner showed up, but I doubt that there's much to find."

He nodded solemnly. "I'll take a look."

"We've got a lead on these guys so George and I are off right now. Keep an eye on Riley. He doesn't look too good."

Harold smiled lightly. "If you are going after these killers you need to be careful. These are not humans who did this. These are vicious animals."

I was going to respond about how much experience I had with these types, but I could see how worried Harold looked. "We'll be careful," I said. I turned and left the apartment.

•   •   •

We had no trouble finding the house that Vera described. It was on Halsted about a quarter of a mile from the Stockyards. It was a ramshackle frame building, pale yellow and in need of repairs. One of the front windows was broken and the roof looked like it had a hole in it. All around the front of the place and on the sides we could see what looked like rusted old farm equipment. The yard leading up to the house was all dirt, dried from the August sun.

We got up to the door which was battered and hanging loosely from the hinges. George stopped me before I knocked. "Undo your holster buckle."

He was right. I reached into my suit and undid the latch. I pounded loudly on the door. I was about to pound again when the door was opened and there stood the man that Vera said reminded her of Satan. He was big through the shoulders and chest with a bald head and black eyes. The thick beard was coal like black. He was wearing a dirty white shirt, untucked, and dusty, worn pants.

"Are you Arnold Perry?" I asked.

"I am," he said. "What is this about?"

"We'd like to talk with you for a minute."

His eyes darted from me to George and back. He looked calm, but tired. "I guess you can come in. It's not much cooler in here, though."

Perry led us into the small house. It was really two rooms, the one that we were in, that had a sitting area and small kitchen space, and a room that had its door closed. I assumed this was a bedroom. Perry sat on an old sofa; George and I remained standing.

"So I got to go to work over at the yards. I was sleeping when you knocked on the door. What do you want with me?"

I looked again at the closed door. "This is where you normally sleep?"

Perry's eyes drifted towards the closed room. "I have a friend who's sick in there. He's still sleeping."

I looked around the small house. It was cluttered with old junk and furniture that was past its time. It was really hot in there. "Do you know a guy named Billy Baxter?"

Perry looked to be pondering this. He was taking a bit too long. "Seems like I know somebody named that. Is there a reason I should know this guy?"

"How about a guy named Finch? To help you out he's missing half on an ear."

He laughed. "I don't know anybody missing half an ear."

"Okay. Getting back to Billy Baxter. Somebody got into his apartment last night and beat him to death. Beat him so badly we couldn't make out his facial features."

"That doesn't sound very good, but I'm not really sure I know this guy."

"Lived above Casey's, second floor. Somebody saw you coming up the stairs there last night just before he was supposedly killed. This person also saw you talking to Billy at the bar on another occasion."

He shook his head. "Don't think anyone saw me. We were here all night. Like I said, my friend is sick in there. We didn't go anywhere?"

He still looked very calm and didn't look like anything was bothering him. "Mind if we talk to your friend for a minute?"

His eyes went to the door and back. "He's really sick and I think he's sleeping?"

"We'll only be a minute or two," I said. "I promise."

We looked at each other for what seemed like a while, but was only seconds. He made a move with his right hand, reaching behind him. I didn't know what hit me, but I was knocked from the side to the floor. I could barely look back when I heard the sound of a revolver being fired at close range. When I was able to look, while on my back, I saw George on one knee, gun extended in both hands, with smoke coming from the barrel. Looking over at Perry, his head was back against the sofa, his white shirt a mass of red. He was clearly dead.

George got off his knee and stood. He put his gun away and gave me a helping hand from the floor. We got close to Perry to see that his right hand held an old thirty-eight. "Guess I should say thanks," I said.

"I don't mind saving your life, Moses, but this is twice now. You owe me a couple."

I patted him on the shoulder. "I'll give you a marker," I said. "What about the sick friend?"

"Let's assume he's like a wounded animal and that he's got a gun. I doubt if he's still sleeping with all of the noise we were making. We'd better think this one out."

I looked down again at the dead Perry. I noticed for the first time that the old, white shirt that he wore was a little dressy for somebody who was a custodian. I saw the glint of gold come from his cuffs. I looked closer and turned the material near his left wrist. He was wearing cuff links, gold ones. They were circular and had two initials engraved in them. They were AP.

"What do you see?" George asked.

"The cufflinks. All gold and engraved. The initials are AP and they are not for Arnold Perry. They are from Allen Price, stolen from him the night he and his family was murdered."

George whistled. "Holy shit!"

"Yeah. Let's figure out what to do with the sick friend."

The room we were in had two windows on the side of the house where the closed bedroom was. We figured there was a third for the bedroom itself.

"You go to the window," I said. "Break it with your gun and then duck. I'll come in the door if whoever is in here starts shooting."

"I'm breaking and ducking," George said. "Try not to kill the bastard so we can get some information."

I gave George a few minutes to get situated outside. I pressed my ear up against the bedroom door waiting for the sound of broken glass. It didn't take long. I heard the glass panes break and not soon after a volley of pistol shots rang out. I opened the door quickly and fired two quick shots at the man who was pointing his gun at the window. The man jerked back in the bed as the bullets hit him and the gun fell out of his hand and onto the floor. I stepped forward and kicked the gun away and looked at the man.

Whoever he was he wasn't related to Arnold Perry. This man had light features, barely any beard growth and straight blonde hair. My shots had hit him in the left shoulder and in the chest on the right side. He wasn't wearing any shirt and I could see where a crude bandage had been previously wrapped around his stomach. This is where Billy Baxter had hit him with the Derringer. The man's eyes fluttered and he looked at me.

"Fucking cop bastard," he said clearly.

I heard George come in behind me. "Doesn't seem dead to me," he said.

"Did Finch put you two up to the Price job and the hit on Billy Baxter?" I asked.

"Fuck you," he said. Blood bubbles started to pop out of his mouth."

I got down close to his face. He grimaced in pain. "We can help you out here, but tell us the truth. Tell me about Price and Baxter."

He was gritting his teeth. "You gotta ask Arnie," he said. Blood ran out of both sides of his mouth.

"Arnie's dead," I said. "Just answer the fucking question."

He looked at me wide eyed. "Fuck you," he said again. He took a tremendous breath, his eyes closed and he slumped to the left.

"Your interviewing talents didn't work very well," George said.

"Arnold Perry was in the Price house, no doubt. Don't know if this character was, but he was there when Billy Baxter got his. I'm pretty sure they are going to find a Derringer bullet in his stomach."

"Look here," George said.

I turned away from the dead man. In the corner of the room, George was standing next to two shotguns that had been stood up in the corner. On the floor by them were boxes of shells.

"These guns and shells will no doubt match up with the ones used at the Price house," George said. "No doubt these are the guys that killed the Prices and Billy Baxter. What do you think about Finch?"

"Well, I'd say are two best witnesses are dead, but maybe there is something here that ties these two to Finch. Even if that isn't the case, we're going to pay him a visit. Right now, we'd better get to a call box and call this in. We've got to get Harold out here to take a look."

"With Billy Baxter and that kid Cyrus, he's had a tough morning."

I looked one more time at the dead guy in the bed. "I'm not sure any rest is coming for any of us very soon."

•　•　•

The door to Finch's home on Princeton was opened by a tiny Chinese man who told us he was the house keeper. He didn't seem too happy that the police were there looking for his boss.

"Mr. Finch, he go on trip," the man said.

"Trip where?" George asked.

"Just trip. Went to Union Station with his lady friend this morning."

"Long ago?" I asked.

"Maybe seven o'clock."

So that was that. Finch had sent his two henchmen to take care of Billy Baxter and to make sure he wasn't looked into had left town. We had no idea where he went and he hadn't even told his house keeper. For now, he was a free man, but coming back into Chicago would be a challenge for him. We would catch up with him eventually.

Back at the precinct things were as chaotic as ever. The news of the Billy Baxter/Cyrus murders had stirred everyone up. Word of the shootout with Arnold Perry and his "sick" friend had already gone through the building and George and I got a bit of a hero's welcome. Lieutenant Shipley came out to the detective's area to greet us. It was the first time I'd seen him smiling in a while.

"You're sure these are the guys who did the Price murders?" he asked.

"One hundred percent. Arnold Perry was wearing gold cufflinks with Allen Price's initials on them. We also found two shotguns and boxes of shells. Harold will look them over and should be able to match them up with casings found at the house."

"And they killed this Billy Baxter character?" Shipley said.

"And the kid named Cyrus. Billy shot one of the guys in the gut with a Derringer. The only problem with this case is that the ring leader Rupert Finch has left town. We'll have to catch up with him at a later date."

Shipley seemed to mull this over for a bit and then he nodded. "At least I can tell Central that we have solved the mystery of who killed Price and his family." He seemed happy that one of our nasty cases had been put to bed. He walked away from us and back towards his office.

On my desk was a message that Jim Colosimo had called for me. At the time, I didn't have the energy to go to Paris to see him so using the department telephone I called him.

"Your boy is still in town, but I don't know where he is," Colosimo said when he came to the phone.

"No idea where, Jim?" I said.

"None, Moses, but I gave my source a message that you were looking for Hanson. He said he could get it to him."

I was quiet for a moment, thinking things out. "Are we done, Moses?" Colosimo asked.

"For now," I said. The line went dead in my hands.

• • •

Before we finished for the day, a message came from Jeremiah Higgins that a meeting with Patricia Farmer's lawyer, Bradley Luke, had been set for eleven in the morning at Luke's loop office. This would give us direction whether Higgins would take the plea deal or press for a trial.

When I finally sat down to dinner at Cooper's, I found that I was both tense and tired. I ordered whiskey and then ordered another. My tension level went down, but my degree of tiredness went up. I wanted so much to have another drink, but I stopped. I also wanted to visit Soon Lee's opium den, but somehow my self- control prevailed. There was nothing left for the day, but home and sleep.

Again, I cautiously moved up the stairs to my apartment. My gun was in my hand the whole way, but somehow I knew this wasn't going to be the way this drama with Christian Hanson ended. When I got to my door, I could see that something else had been put on it. It was a piece of paper. I took it off the small nail and moved into the better light in my unit. The note was only a short sentence. I knew who had sent it.

I'LL BE SEEING YOU VERY SOON, MOSES.

The tightness at the base of my neck returned. Colosimo had delivered a message. It had been answered. My temples throbbed. I wasn't afraid for me. I was afraid because I figured Hanson would do something to someone else to draw me out. I sat in my small living room chair for quite a while with the note in my hand.

Day Twelve

Bradley Luke's office was located on Adams Street just a little west of State Street. I was relieved to find that the office was located on the first floor. My relationship with elevators was tenuous and I didn't need any more stress to start my day. As it was, the office was very nice and projected a professional atmosphere. Having met Luke, I thought we might be dealing with something less than professional.

The conference room we were in made our meeting rooms at the precinct look like dungeons. There was a long table of well- polished wood and eight matching chairs. A young woman brought in a pitcher of cold water with glasses that may have been crystal. Luke's firm, no doubt, was doing okay.

When he entered the room he looked surprised to find myself and George in the room. "You've brought some friends with you, Jeremiah?"

Higgins smiled. "A little backup," he said.

Luke wasn't smiling. He stood for a moment, quietly looking at us. Dressed in a dark blue suit that contrasted his pale skin, I thought for a moment he might ask us to leave, but he just sat down. "You called this meeting, Jeremiah, so why don't we move it along."

"I'm afraid that the plea offer that you have made is insufficient to make amends for Miss Farmer's crimes," the young prosecutor said.

Luke laughed, a very small laugh. "My client has confessed to being there during the commission of the crimes. She has said that she did nothing physical to any of the murdered women. She has also stated that she did draw some pencil sketches while at the crime scene. That is our reason why we will ask the judge for leniency in his sentencing. To compliment this plea and request, we understand that Miss Marsden has confessed to killing the women and also has stated that Patricia Farmer did nothing. I don't see that our plea is insufficient to make amends."

Now I remembered what I didn't like about Luke. It was his smug, confident way of talking to you, trying to put you on the defensive, trying to make you feel small.

"Bradley, "Jeremiah said evenly, "we've learned quite a few things about Miss Farmer during our investigation. She has a long history, at least what we could find so far, of coercing people to do bad things for her in return for promises."

Luke sat back in his chair. "Don't try and bluff me."

"No bluff. Detective Moses, would you please inform Mr. Luke briefly what you have found?"

I cleared my throat and took a sip of the cold water. For some reason, I felt nervous. "It appears that the relationship between Madeline Marsden and Patricia Farmer is the third time that Patricia has talked somebody else into doing bad things for her. One was in St. Louis that caused the Farmer family to move here. Another was on the north side that forced Patricia to transfer to St. Regina. The third involved Madeline Marsden.

"Two of the incidents involved weaker girls. Patricia promised friendship to these girls in exchange for being friends. Once the evil deeds were committed, Patricia Farmer pulled away from these girls, claiming innocence. In the other case, she promised a young boy love, and other things. The young boy beat up another boy, was caught and punished. Patricia claimed total innocence, even though many heard her coax the young boy to do what he did. It's our belief that Miss Farmer is a skilled manipulator. None of these crimes would have been committed without her convincing others to act on her behalf."

Luke leaned back and crossed his arms across his chest. "That is the best you could do, detective?"

"We have a number of witnesses in each case, willing to testify at a trial," I said. I felt the tension in my neck and temples.

"Is this what this meeting is all about, Jeremiah? Are you telling me you will reject our plea and demand a trial?" Luke's face showed color for the first time.

"Quite frankly, Bradley, we see Miss Farmer as a menace. Giving her a light sentence would put her back on the street in too short a period of time for that to be a benefit to anyone."

Luke laughed. "So you want her to plead to murder one charges?"

Jeremiah smiled. "At least murder two."

"Not possible," Luke said loudly. "Patricia Farmer did nothing with respect to the actual murders. Miss Marsden admits to doing everything. I don't think your three cases, as you call them, of manipulation will hold much water. As a matter of fact, they sound rather fanciful. Nothing in the law addresses anything like that or calls for any punishment. That's why I maintain that this is just a bluff. I see no reason to recall our plea and would be more than willing to go to a trial. If nothing else, I'd be looking forward to the judge listening to Detective Moses' enlightening story and then laughing you all out of the courthouse."

Jeremiah Higgins said nothing at first. If he felt like I did, he got the sense that Luke was not going to back down and was supremely confident in his defense of Patricia Farmer.

"I will refer the matter to my superiors and will advise," Jeremiah said. "At this time, I will put your plea on hold until I hear more. I just want to warn you that during a trial some nasty and potentially harmful details about Patricia Farmer and her past may be revealed."

Luke got a very disdainful look on his face. "This is not my first case nor would it be my first trial. These threats of making people look bad work both ways."

In the lobby of the building, I could tell none of us was feeling very good about the meeting.

"That didn't seem very productive," George said.

"Very astute, Detective Loftus," Higgins said. "I will go upstairs and present where we are and what we have and see what the outcome is."

"Your initial thoughts?" I asked.

Jeremiah looked at me. "Trials are very long sometimes and costly. There is also the possibility that we might lose. We have, in hand, a confession to a crime, a much lesser one than murder. Upstairs might say that is good enough. Patricia Farmer does get convicted and will spend some time somewhere other than her home. That may be the best we get."

George and I looked at each other. We'd been on the case for a while and it looked like we would know the outcome in a short time frame. I didn't understand the law and never understood judges so I had no idea how this would end up. I did know that Jeremiah Higgins' last words to us did not provide much encouragement for seeing a greater sentence for Patricia Farmer.

• • •

With the less than good news we received from our meeting with Bradley Luke, I found myself in a position where I felt there wasn't much I could do. Arnold Perry and his still unidentified friend were the hitmen for the Prices, Billy Baxter and Cyrus. I didn't doubt that they had been financed by the half- eared Rupert Finch, but he was gone and we probably wouldn't see him for a while. I also knew that Christian Hanson was playing a game with me, using street patrolmen as pieces. I only hoped he wouldn't kill someone else. I hoped he would move onto the next phase of the game. I knew this would be the most dangerous step, but it had to happen. I also knew that he wanted it. We were due for a showdown. I was ready.

I wandered down to the basement to see if Harold Pinter was around. I hadn't seen him since the scene at the small house on Halsted Street. A good part of me just wanted to make sure he was doing okay.

As usual, Harold had his head down, peering at something on his desk. I knocked and he looked up and smiled.

"Ah, Patrick, I am glad you stopped by," he said, smiling.

"Good news?" I asked.

"No real news. Just confirmation. The shotgun casings that we found at the Price home matched those in the box at the house on

Halsted. There were also several pieces of jewelry found in the house. I'm pretty sure that we can get somebody to confirm that these pieces belonged to Mrs. Price. Mr. Arnold and his friend were the Price murderers. I'm also certain that when a bullet is extracted from the friend we will be able to confirm that it was fired from Billy Baxter's Derringer."

"That is all good news," I said.

"But you don't look very happy."

"It seems we are at an impasse on Patricia Farmer. Her lawyer was not impressed with all of the information that we presented about her manipulating talents and our threat of going to trial didn't shake him."

"So there will be a trial?"

"I don't know. Jeremiah Higgins wasn't sure his superiors would want to put on a trial when they had a confession and a conviction in hand. He felt they may just stay with that and move on."

Harold shook his head and straightened his glasses which had slipped down his nose. "The Marsden girl still maintains that she did all of the physical dirty work?"

"Every bit of it. It's unbelievable the spell she is under. She doesn't want to do anything that will upset her friendship with Patricia."

"What kind of sentence will Patricia Farmer get?"

"Jeremiah isn't sure, but he thinks it won't even be close to what fits the magnitude of the crime. We're pretty sure Madeline will stay in the Children's Home until she is eighteen and then be moved to County. Patricia won't be dealing with any of that."

Harold seemed to think for a minute. "Nothing more you can do?"

"We've played every card we have."

He nodded. "Let me think on that for a bit," he said.

"How is Martha?"

Harold's look saddened. "She had a very tough night last night. She is getting very close to the end; her breathing is not strong. I fear we are getting close."

"Don't you want to be there?"

"She would understand, Patrick. She would understand that I have work to do and I can no longer be of any help to her."

He looked so worn out talking about it. "Any word from your son in Denver?"

"I have sent another telegram. I haven't heard anything as of yet."

"You'll let me know if you need anything?"

"Of course I will. Patrick, promise you'll be careful out there. I don't like some of the things you get mixed up in. I also think that your friend Christian Hanson epitomizes evil."

I smiled. "I'll be careful. My job is to tame evil. I know it's coming, but I don't know when. I just have to be ready to confront it."

Harold's look showed that he didn't have much confidence in that statement. He returned his look to whatever he had been studying when I showed up. I left his little office.

As I was coming up the stairs I ran into Lieutenant Shipley as he was headed out of the building. He wore an actual smile when he saw me. "Moses, excellent work on the Price case. A great piece of police work."

I didn't consider a tip from woman in a bar to be great police work. "We got a little lucky."

He looked surprised. "Anything on your search for Hanson?"

"I'm trying to locate the bastard"

His smile returned. "Close that one out and it will be a great week."

"I'll do my best," I said.

Shipley turned and proceeded out of the building. I felt sorry for him. We had to contend with a few cases in the Levee. He was responsible for all of them.

•　　•　　•

I had barely sat down for my dinner at Cooper's when a woman approached my table and sat down. She was wearing a dark dress and a black scarf covered her head. When she raised her head to look at me I could see some of the curls under the scarf. The bruising and swelling had subsided a bit, but were still present on her face.

"We need your help right away, Detective Moses," Annie Grimes said.

"Were you waiting for me here?" I asked.

"I was told that you come here every night," she said, "but we have no time for idle chatter."

I wondered what the rush was and also wondered if a prostitute could track me how tough could it be. "Tell me what the issue is."

"It's Joan McDermott. Your friend Jack Garfield came to see her."

"Tonight?" It was only a little past eight.

"Within the last hour. You have to come now."

We caught a carriage out front and I told the driver to get us to The Bitter End quickly. There was some traffic in the streets at this hour, but we made good time. I followed Annie up the stairs and into the brothel. I noticed that the place was eerily silent. Mrs. Flint looked as if she's seen a ghost when I saw her in the lobby.

"Quiet night?" I asked.

"Closed for the night, Detective. Annie, take him upstairs," she said.

I followed Annie up the stairs to the second floor. There were no sounds in the old building. We entered the second room on the right. Joan McDermott was sitting in a chair near the bed. The room was well lit. Joan had a welt under her left eye and a split lip. Blood also could be seen near her right ear. There was blood on her bosom and down the front on her night dress. She looked at me and tears welled in her eyes.

I was going to go right to her, but gazed upon the bed. There in a stage of undress was the body of Jack Garfield. He looked to be resting with his arms at his side. His head was back and his eyes were closed; his mouth hung open. I'd say he was peaceful other than the four inch blade, one with a handle I recognized, that was protruding from just below his throat. Joan had taken a few lumps from Captain Jack, but had evened the score with the little knife.

"He came after you?" I asked.

She nodded as tears rolled down her face. "He started asking about you," she said. "I told him I knew nothing and he started to hit me. I was able to get the knife from the drawer. I didn't mean to kill him."

I looked again at where the knife had been stuck into the captain. Stabbing someone in the throat was probably a bad defense for saying you weren't trying to kill him. "It was self- defense."

"What are we going to do, Patrick?" she pleaded.

My feelings for Jack Garfield were similar to those I felt for rats along Clark Street after midnight. If I had my way I'd dump him in the Chicago River and call it even, but I was going to play this the right way. I told the girls to sit tight and I went back downstairs. Mrs. Flint had a telephone and I called the precinct. I told them to find George Loftus and to get ahold of Prosecutor Jeremiah Higgins. My message to both men was to meet me at The Bitter End.

Loftus got to the brothel at nine-fifteen; it wasn't that much later that Jeremiah showed up. I told George I would explain what was going on when the lawyer showed up. When Higgins appeared, he didn't seem very happy.

"This had better be good, Moses. I was with a very lovely lady," Higgins said.

"This will be more excitement than you have had in a long while."

I led the two of them upstairs and to Joan's room. I opened the door and George went in first, followed by Higgins.

"Holy shit!" George said.

"Oh, my goodness," Higgins said. He didn't notice the two women in the room.

"Know him?" I asked.

Higgins got a little closer and took a better look. "I believe that is Black Jack Garfield," he said.

"It is," I said. "He was killed in self-defense by Miss McDermott. She is the dark haired young lady. She was attacked by Captain Jack and responded. The other young woman is Annie Grimes. She had been recently attacked by Jack, but didn't have a knife to defend herself."

Jeremiah turned and faced the two prostitutes. He surveyed their injuries which were clear to see. "Is what Detective Moses said to me the truth?"

"Yes, sir," the two said in unison.

He shook his head. "I'm sorry that one of our officers treated you so poorly. I hope that neither one of you suffered badly. The case is clear, though. This is a case of self -defense. I don't think it will end here in this room. The Police Department doesn't handle the death of Captains very well so I'm sure that you both will have to give a statement in the very near future. I will make sure that I set that up for you. For now, we need to get a coroner's van here and get Captain Garfield out of Bed Bug Row."

As we waited for the coroner in the lobby of the brothel, Jeremiah Higgins pulled me aside. "Why would these two prostitutes call you after killing Captain Garfield?"

I smiled. "We're friends," I said.

"That's it?"

"The Captain has never liked me. That is common knowledge. When he beat up Annie, I told them to call if he ever did anything like that again. They called, but it was a bit too late for Jack."

Jeremiah looked at me for a minute. "I met with my people upstairs this afternoon. They'll let me know soon about our case with Patricia Farmer and the plea deals, probably tomorrow."

"Your thoughts?"

"Cross your fingers," he said.

When Garfield was loaded in the coroner's van and George and Jeremiah had gone home, I was ready to go home myself. I was hungry and tired, a bad combination, but also relieved. We knew who had killed Allen Price and we knew who put them up to it. My feud with Jack Garfield had also ended quickly. Two weights had been lifted from my shoulder. The outcome of the Old Lady Murders would be the third case to come to an end. That only left Hanson and the two murdered patrolmen. I shuddered.

I was about to walk out the door when Joan McDermott came down the stairs. She had cleaned up and changed her clothes. Her lip looked okay, but the bruise on her face was not going to be pretty. She came up to me and kissed me on the cheek.

"What was that for?" I asked.

She kissed me lightly on the lips. "I'm sorry. I treated you poorly and you didn't deserve it. I wanted to apologize to you."

"Apology accepted."

"And to ask you for another chance."

I stared into her dark eyes. Even with a cracked lip and a black eye, she was so pretty. "Can I think about it?"

I saw her face flush. "Patrick Moses!"

I kissed her this time. "I'm pretty sure we can work something out," I said.

I walked home in the warm night air. The Levee was bustling and noisy, but I heard nothing. My mind was totally clear and I was relaxed. There could be only one reason for this. I was happy. It had been a long time since I felt this way. I didn't know how long it would last, but it felt good. It had been a long time.

Day Thirteen

It was just a little past ten the next day when Shipley called myself, George and Harold Pinter into his office on the second floor. I couldn't get much of a read on the Lieutenant. He looked calm sitting behind his desk. The bottle of bromide tablets was sitting on the desk, but was not opened. None of us took a seat in the chairs that were available.

Shipley looked at me. "You had an interesting night, Detective Moses."

"A better night than Captain Garfield."

"I'm sure this won't be the last time we discuss this issue, but for now we have other things to discuss."

"We can't do much for the Captain," I said. Shipley smiled weakly.

"I suppose I have some good news and maybe some that is not so good," Shipley said. "I have just heard from Attorney Higgins. He called me in order to follow proper protocol."

I didn't care one way or another about protocol. "Why don't you give us the good news first?" I said.

He picked up a piece of paper where he had written some notes. "The state has accepted the guilty plea of Murder One for Madeline Marsden. She will remain in the Children's Home until the age of eighteen. At that time she will be transferred to county where she will serve an additional twenty years to life."

I took a deep breath and gritted my teeth. "That doesn't sound like good news for Madeline."

"A young girl, but a murderer," Shipley said.

"The bad news?" I asked.

"The state has also accepted the plea that was presented by Patricia Farmer's attorney. Miss Farmer will remain on strict probation until the age of eighteen. She will be remanded to Saint Mary's School for Girls in Milwaukee. At that time she will be released."

"She gets to go to some plushy girl's school while Madeline goes to prison?" I said.

"I didn't think you'd care for that," Shipley said. "Apparently Mr. Farmer has some very good connections and Bradley Luke, the attorney, was able to convince the judge that this was the proper place for her to spend her confinement. The school is supposedly very strict. The judge was also working with one girl being a cold killer and the other drawing some pictures."

"We all know that isn't true," I said loudly.

"Moses, you guys did a great job. You got two convictions, but when one person says they did all of the dirty work and says the other person did next to nothing, it's hard for a judge to throw hard sentences at both people."

I was upset, but not surprised. Jeremiah Higgins said that something of this nature might happen. He had been correct.

"Now, if we can close out the Kell and Bourne murders, maybe we can move onto some different things," Shipley said.

I didn't comment. I turned and walked out of the office with George and Harold behind me. As I got close to my desk, Harold grabbed my arm. George sat down on my desk. "Forget about it Patrick," George said. "This was all decided by people who are a lot higher up than we are."

"George is right," Harold said. "There's not a damn thing you can do about it."

I nodded and decided they were both right. Both of the girls were mentally unhinged as far as I could tell. It just bothered me that Patricia Farmer got such a better deal.

"I have talked to a friend of mine," Harold said. "He runs a work camp, men and women, outside of Louisville, Kentucky. They have a section that works with teenagers that are problem children."

I wanted to make sure that I understood what Harold was saying. When I looked into his sad eyes, he only nodded at me.

We hadn't been out of the meeting with Shipley very long when we got word that there was a problem at the home of Detective Riley O'Donnell. Riley was a tough old cop. He had been on the force over twenty years. He lived in a small house over in Pilsen with his wife and four kids. George and I went to the vehicle pool and there was an auto available. It didn't take us long to get out to Pilsen.

The O'Donnell house was small and well kept. If you looked at it this morning you got the impression that all was well. There was a neat little lawn, some bushes and blooming flowers. We pulled up in front and made our way to the front door.

Riley answered the door and immediately I knew something was bad. Riley always looked older than he was with his receding hairline and bulging waistline. Today he added a pale skin tone and eyes that looked like they had been crying or hadn't slept in days.

"Riley, what the hell is it?" I asked.

He grabbed me by both shoulders. "It's my boy, Danny, eight years old. Somebody took him."

His grip was hurting my arms. "What do you mean somebody took him?"

"Come on," Riley said, taking his hands off me and leading us into the house.

Riley's wife and three daughters were sitting in a small living area. They all had their heads down and it was clear they were not in a good way. We walked past them with no words spoken. Riley led us to the back of the house. There was a small room there with a tiny bed. To the left of this room was a door leading to a yard in the back. It was partially open.

"This is Danny's room. He sleeps alone because he's the only boy. The three girls sleep in the other bedroom. Somebody came in here last night and took him. He was gone when Sandra looked in on him this morning."

"How do you know he just didn't go out to play or do something, Riley?" George asked. His tone was trying to calm Riley down.

"Because of this," Riley said. He handed me a small, white envelope. My name was scrawled across the front of it. "I didn't open it."

I looked down at the envelope and my hand shook a bit. I knew the handwriting. I opened the envelope and took out the paper that was inside of it.

MOSES, I HAVE THE BOY. CUTE KID. CLARK STREET PIER AT MIDNIGHT. DON'T BRING ANY OF YOUR PALS OR I'LL KILL HIM. JUST ME AND YOU. I KNOW YOU ARE A MAN OF SOME HONOR AND WILL FOLLOW THE RULES. I WILL KILL HIM WITH A KNIFE IF YOU FUCK WITH ME.

"What does it say?" Riley asked.

"I know who has your son, Riley and I'm going to get him back. It's Christian Hanson."

"My God," Riley said. "He took my Danny to get back at you? How could you let this happen, Patrick?"

I had no words for Riley to answer that one. The only response would be that I'd had my chances to kill Hanson, but had failed to do so. "I'll get Danny back," I said.

I turned and left the house with George trailing behind me. I didn't divulge what was in the letter from Hanson to Riley. I didn't say anything to George Loftus.

"How are you going to get the boy back?" George asked.

"I only know where he's going to be with Danny. I haven't figured out how to do anything yet."

"Well, I'll go with you."

"Won't work. I've got to go alone. If Hanson sees any other cops, he will kill the boy instantly. Right now drop me at my apartment. I need to think and be ready."

"This is crazy, Patrick."

I grabbed Loftus like Riley had grabbed me. "Not a fucking word about this to anyone, George. Hanson will kill that boy if we fuck up at all. This is between me and him. That's it. This is a showdown."

"You're fucking as crazy as Hanson."

The words stung, but George was right. In a way we were both killers. I had killed some men, but these were evil doers. Hanson had killed innocent people and seemed to like doing it. That was the big difference. "Maybe," I said, "but I'm going to get Danny O'Donnell back."

• • •

I had only been to the Clark Street pier once in my life and that had been to find little Freddie Winston tied to a pole, naked and shivering. Christian Hanson had taken Freddie and now he had taken Danny O'Donnell. With Freddie it had been a tactic to scare me. I wasn't sure what Hanson was up to now, but he had found a way to get me out into the open.

The night had cooled significantly from the day's heat. It left a fog rising off the Chicago River as I approached the pier from the east. The moonless night left little light to see by. I made my way towards the pole where Freddie had been tied up. I got to within fifty feet of it.

"Far enough, Moses," a voice said.

The voice startled me. Hanson was a mute. The moon popped out just as a man stepped out from behind a shed to my left. I couldn't make out much, but I could see the golden hair.

I remembered my dream from the past where I had shot Hanson and killed him. He had spoken in the dream. "You can't talk," I said.

"Oh, I can talk," he said. "I used the mute practice once and it worked, but I can talk perfectly fine."

There was no accent to the voice. "Where's the boy?" I asked.

"Soon Moses. Soon. Right now I need you to do something." He raised his right arm and I saw he was holding a large revolver. "I need you to take out your gun and throw it in the river."

"Show me the boy and let him go," I said.

He moved to my left and walked along the edge of the river. There were some poles there where boats could moor. It was then that I saw Danny O'Donnell. He was tied to a mooring pole with a hood over his head. Hanson, still covering me, walked to the pole and lifted the hood off of Danny. I took a few steps in that direction.

"I said close enough," Hanson said.

Now I could see Danny pretty well. He was tied to the pole tightly and was gagged. He didn't look harmed in any way. Hanson got close to him and with his other hand drew a knife from his pocket. He switched his gun into the other hand. He stuck the tip of the knife under Danny's left eye.

"Come on, Hanson. This is between you and me," I said.

"Your gun in the next ten seconds or the boy loses the eye."

Danny's head started to shake a bit and I knew he was crying. Hanson's gun was leveled at my chest. At this range it would blow a good sized hole in me.

"Last chance, Moses," he said.

I drew my service revolver out of its holster and threw it into the river. Hanson let out a shriek like and animal and smiled broadly. He put the knife back in his pocket and approached me. He stopped about twenty feet away. I had a better view. The golden hair wasn't parted down the middle. His gun was still pointed at me.

"I respect that you are a man of your word and I respect that you know how to follow rules. Other than that I find you to be a piece of shit," he said.

"I'm having a very hard time forgetting what you did to those girls in Blue Island. I don't know how to describe you, but all I can say is that you are not human. You are the definition of evil."

He laughed. "The devil, Satan?"

"Close to the truth," I said.

"Well, I'm glad we were able to confirm our feelings for each other, but now I think it is time for us to move along. One of us must die and I'm afraid it is you, Moses. By the way, I will kill the boy after you are gone. I'm going to kill you now, but it's not going to be quick. I'm going to take my time and enjoy it."

I don't know why, but I closed my eyes. There was a simultaneous explosion of his gun and a hard impact to my left shoulder. The pain was excruciating and I was knocked to the ground. The slug had clearly broken bones. I opened my eyes and Hanson was walking towards me. He had holstered the gun. A surge of pain ran through me. I was close to passing out.

"You are so fucking stupid, Moses. Truly, maybe the dumbest cop I had ever met." He took the knife back out of his pocket. "This should be fun."

I took a deep breath. My shoulder was in bad shape. I might be stupid, but I wasn't the dumbest cop alive. I had dealt with enough crooks to know better. I was able to reach into my pocket on my right side and find the throw away I had stashed earlier. It was a well- oiled, snub-nosed, thirty-eight.

I looked up into his eyes as he approached. The moon made an appearance and glanced off the six inch blade. The gleam in his eyes was more pronounced. He looked possessed. "It's been fun, Moses," he said.

My vision was blurring, but he was so close. I angled the gun inside of my pocket and fired. The bullet hit Hanson just below the throat. He stumbled backward and fell onto the ground. The knife clattered away. I wasn't long for being alert, but I managed to crawl to Hanson. He was lying on his back, hands to his wound. I got up beside him and looked into his eyes. He locked eyes with me and gritted his teeth.

"You cheated, you bastard" he said.

"Sorry," I said. I raised the thirty-eight and placed the barrel in his left ear. "Time to go." I fired and a good portion of Hanson's brain came out of the other side of his head. The impact of the bullet rocked his head and the blonde hair fell away, another wig. The man I had killed had short dark hair. It wasn't Hanson at all. I shook my head. I was barely conscious. I had one more thing to do.

I crawled to the knife and then I crawled over to where Danny was tied up. He was still sobbing. I got to my knees and cut the lower bindings. "Danny, quiet," I said. He looked at me and I think realized he was safe. Grabbing the pole for support, I pulled myself up and cut the higher bindings and the gag off his mouth. I fell to one knee.

"What do I need to do?" I heard him say.

I pointed to the stairs in the distance. "Get up there. Find someone, anyone."

I slumped to the ground and the last sound I remember was the sound of Danny's feet running towards the steps.

In The End

I spent five days at Mercy. The nice nurse who I'd met while visiting Martha Pinter kept an eye on me and got me extra laudanum when the pain got to be too much. The bullet that the Christian Hanson impersonator got me with cracked a bone in my shoulder, restricting my arm motion. The doctor was able to extract the bullet and patch me up. The biggest concern had been the loss of blood. That had been what had knocked me down. During my drug induced rest I had many visitors, but talked to only a few, I think. Harold came with George Loftus. Riley was there with Danny. Shipley came and I remember wishing he would leave. Lastly, Joan McDermott was there on a daily basis.

On the sixth day, I got word that Martha Pinter had died a couple of days before. On this day there would be a funeral service at Resurrection Cemetery. Against doctor's orders, I was going to attend. I got Joan to help get me dressed and out of the bed. My first steps were not great and I thought I might pass out, but I adjusted and got stronger with each step. George was waiting downstairs with an auto and we all drove to the cemetery.

It was a cloud covered day with a light mist falling. The temperature had finally cooled. We all stood close by and listened to the priest say the final words for Martha Pinter. I was glad that Shipley made it out. Riley was there as well with his whole family. There were many people I didn't know. This didn't surprise me. I thought a man like Harold, and his wife, would have many friends.

What I noticed the most was the man that stood next to Harold and had his arm around him. A better view showed me a younger version of Harold. His son had made it home from Denver. Next to the son, with his hand on the son's shoulder, was another younger man. I felt terrible for a woman, Martha Pinter, that I had never met, but I felt good for Harold. It had been a long time since I'd felt the feeling of family, but I had a glimpse.

I looked into Joan's eyes as she rested her head on my shoulder. "Thank you," I said quietly.

"For what?" she asked.

"For staying by me," I said.

When the service ended and we were heading back to the auto, George grabbed me lightly by the shoulder. "Go home. Get some rest. I will pick you up at eight tonight."

I laughed. "I have no idea what shape I'll be in. Where are we going?"

He returned the smile. "It's a surprise for you."

George picked me up at precisely eight o'clock. He said nothing about where we were headed, but as we got towards the western part of the city I had an idea. We pulled into a section of the alley behind the Cook County Home for Wayward Children.

"What's going on George?" I asked.

Just then a state vehicle arrived at the back door of the home. A lone attendant got out of the auto and went into the home. It was only moments before he returned. He was leading the way for Patricia Farmer. I looked over at George.

"She's being transferred to the girl's school tonight," he said. "Train leaves in an hour. Her parents will be at the station."

When the man had Patricia situated in the back seat of the auto, he said something to her and reentered the building, leaving her alone.

"That's my signal," George said and he stepped out of our auto.

He quickly approached the state vehicle as another auto pulled up beside it. The driver got out of the car. It was Johnny Allard. George went up to the side of the auto where Patricia was seated and yanked the door open. He grabbed her by the arm and pulled her out. He forced a hood over the surprised girl. Allard opened the rear door of his auto and helped push Patricia into the back seat of that car. George got in beside her and Johnny returned to the driver's seat. The car soon sped off down the alley and into the night.

The driver's door to my left opened and Riley O'Donnell got in and pulled away from the alley.

"Riley, what in the hell is going on?" I said.

"Patricia Farmer is being transferred tonight, but not to that Catholic school in Milwaukee. Mr. Pinter arranged for his friend in Louisville to find a spot for her on his work farm. George got Johnny Allard and paid him fifty dollars to be the driver. We all chipped in for the cost. George will be out a few days. I'm to take you home and put you to bed. You're on vacation."

"What happened to the driver of the state car?"

"Forgot the order inside, I guess," Riley said. "Had to go in and get it."

"A work farm?" I said out loud.

"She won't harm too many people down there," Riley said.

I laughed. "If she messes with anyone down there someone might take it out on her."

"That's the idea, Patrick. That's the whole idea."

I laughed, but then I remembered. A man had dressed like Christian Hanson and had tried to kill me. Another case of someone manipulating someone else. I shivered. This meant that Hanson, and his evil ways were still out there. There was also Rupert Finch. He was out there, too. While trying to tame evil, I had left two big purveyors of it out there. They would both be back in the Levee at some time. The Levee was the home of evil.

The End

About the Author

John Sturgeon is the author of three books in the *Levee District* series. He is also the author of *The Murder of Fatty Fuller*. John lives in Wheaton, Illinois and Sarasota, Florida with his wife Mary.

Note from the Author

Word-of-mouth is crucial for any author to succeed. If you enjoyed *Taming Evil*, please leave a review online—anywhere you are able. Even if it's just a sentence or two. It would make all the difference and would be very much appreciated.

Thanks!
John Sturgeon

Thank you so much for reading one of John Sturgeon's novels.
If you enjoyed the experience, please check out Book One of the
Levee District series for your next great read!

Crimes of the Levee by John Sturgeon

"This series is perfect for fans of historical crime!"
-Anne Bonny Book Reviews

View other Black Rose Writing titles at
www.blackrosewriting.com/books and use promo code
PRINT to receive a **20% discount** when purchasing.